The Darkling Beasts

The Darklling Beasts
© Copyright 2013 Reg Down

ISBN 13: 978-1490392431
ISBN 10: 1490392432

All rights reserved. No part of this book may be reproduced in any form or by any means without the written prior permission of the author, except for brief quotations embodied in critical articles for review.

Lightly Press
lightlypress@gmail.com

Cover: Reg Down

30 May 2016

The Darkling Beasts

Reg Down

~ CONTENTS ~

Prologue 7
1 - Carnival 8
2 - Cam 11
3 - Cam's Mum 13
4 - Cam's Mum's Place 14
5 - Gopher Throw 16
6 - Two Cats 19
7 - Siggy Stands 20
8 - Perkiomenville 21
9 - Hotel Ritz 24
10 - Alf the Barker 26
11 - Doyen of Fashion 29
12 - The Man 32
13 - Other Place 33
14 - Night 38
15 - Pyramid 41
16 - Night Forest 47
17 - Back 51
18 - Chosen One 54
19 - Two Meals 56
20 - Instar 57
21 - Orange and Meat 60
22 - To the Sea 62
23 - Swimming 64
24 - Stranded 67
25 - Back to Shore 69
26 - Meeting 71
27 - Ester tells 74
28 - Materials 76

29 - Gone 81

30 - Sanctum 82

31 - Escape 88

32 - Truth 90

33 - First Battle 93

34 - Farlin 96

35 - Slug of Gold 99

36 - Stymie 104

37 - Skirmish 105

38 - Morning 107

39 - Survivor 110

40 - Counter Tactics 112

41 - Alf's World 114

42 - Siblings 119

43 - Battle at Nova 121

44 - Aftermath 125

45 - Siggy appears 127

46 - Felling 131

47 - Death of a King 136

48 - Night at the Pyramid 144

49 - Brooding Ground 148

50 - Octahedron 151

51 - Winds of Change 156

52 - Arrested 159

53 - Parenting Style 162

54 - Escape 165

55 - To and Fro 167

56 - Burning 172

57 - Lawyer 173

58 - A new Nest 175

Prologue

Alf was an odd child. Odd, however, only in the sense that he was more or less normal in an odd family. His parents, Jack and Jill Upton-Hill, (yes, really) were artists and subscribed to Laissez Faire. Both, that is. Both the magazine and the philosophy of doing whatever they liked as long as there were no hassles. It seemed to work for Jack and Jill and nothing bad had happened, so far.

And likewise for Alf, so far.

Alf, as I said, was odd in that he was normal. His other oddness was that he had an invisible friend. In the young child this is usual, but culture quickly stops allowing such things after the age of three or four. Not Jack and Jill. They found it proof positive that their son, Alfred Singworthy Upton-Hill, had the genius of fantasy abundant. They encouraged him, believed him, and defended him in public when he talked to his invisible friend at the age of five, seven, nine ... and so forth until Alf's current twelfth year—his first zodiac, as his mother enthusiastically called it, presenting him (in the presence of his classmates) with a birthday cake hosting all twelve signs sculpted and painted in pink and green icing.

Alf's invisible friend, whose formal name was unpronounceable, being in Elvench, called himself, when pushed, Singular Elf. Alf (and thus his parents) called him Siggy. By curious happenstance Alf's proper name, Alfred, means 'elf council', and was thus tangentially appropriate to their friendship.

Alf and Siggy were inseparable, and Alf could often be heard in his bedroom (door closed) talking for hours on end on the most unusual subjects. Siggy, you see, was intelligent. Quite. On occasion Siggy also used magic of a weak and trivial sort, such as smudging Jill's lipstick or causing Jack to call his doting wife Sandy. Jill then glared at Jack and Alf fell over himself laughing as his dad tried to extricate himself, only to make things worse by apologizing to Sandy and not Jill. Neither parent believed that Siggy could do such things, but they were wrong. Truth be told, they didn't think Siggy was really real either, but here again they were wrong.

Then the financial crisis of the late noughties hit. Jack and Jill were tossed out of their house upon Forrest Heights by the bank. Later, it turned out that the paperwork was fraudulent and their payments manipulated.

Having a laissez faire philosophy Jack and Jill didn't have any choice but to let banks be banks and do what they wished. Jill, however, wept a tear. She couldn't understand how the intelligent people heading up the banks could generate such bad karma. Surely they understood they'd suffer their creation, if not in this life, then after death and/or in their next incarnation. Didn't they perceive the iron law of necessity? Being kindhearted, she failed to see that the banking industry was riddled with genuine, dyed-in-the-wool sociopaths who recognized in money the perfect means to screw people up for years on end.

After being unceremoniously dumped out of their house and onto the lawn, Jack and Jill rented a granny suite behind a dilapidated working class house in Mainsfield and continued to pursue art. The sofa in the living room became Alf's bedroom and was curtained off for privacy. Alf didn't mind, much, being used to playing outside most of the day. The rest of the living room was a painting and sculpting studio, and the kitchen was for dying wool and fabric and, occasionally, preparing meals.

This was the situation when the carnival came to town. Alf had finished school for the year and was bored. The summer loomed in an unfamiliar and unfriendly neighborhood. Jill decided that a few dollars spent on candy floss and roundabouts would do Alf good.

"Can Siggy come too?" asked Alf.

Jill rolled her eyes.

"Of course he can, sweetie."

So off they went.

1 – *Carnival*

The carnival blared, the lights blinked, the people crowded, and the homeless dug into trash cans. Alf ran into a few classmates from his old school and hung out with them until it began to get late. Alf didn't have a bedtime but they were hauled off home. After eating candy floss and caramel apples and taking a dozen more rides he begged to go into the Hall of Mirrors. The Hall was unimposing; a jaded trailer hosted by a beer belly, but in the colored lights it looked inviting to Alf.

"Off you go then," said his dad, giving him a dollar for the ticket. "But that's the last thing. Meet us over by the big wheel."

So in Alf went with Siggy in tow. The Hall was made up of narrow passages lined with floor-to-ceiling mirrors laid out in a maze. Soon Alf was lost and trying to find his way out the other side. Everywhere he looked he saw images of himself retreating into infinity and Alf's young mind was impressed. Siggy was bored to tears, but seeing how deliciously confusing the mirrors were to Alf he decided to set a binding spell. It was just a piece of fun. You know, 'binding' as in keep-the-victim-going-round-and-round-in-one-place-ha-ha-ha kind of spell.

Siggy chanted appropriately in Elvench:

which, loosely translated, means:

> *"Higgelty-piggelty-dangle,*
> *Tie him in a tangle!"*

Poof!—the magic bounced around the mirrors and tied Siggy up.

The problem lay in the him. In the spell, that is: tie *him* in a tangle. Siggy meant 'him' as in Alf, but the spell looked around for someone other than Siggy and found it in Siggy's thousand-fold reflection everywhere in the mirrors. Confused, the spell took the easiest route and tangled the whole lot up, including Siggy's actual self. Now he was trapped.

The magic affected Alf too, but in the intended way. It bounced zip-zap around the Hall of Mirrors and Alf couldn't find his way out of the maze. After fifteen minutes Alf had had enough of the Hall. After half an hour he began to worry.

"Siggy! Siggy! Where are you?" Alf cried, hoping Siggy would know the way out.

"Hermm mmm mm m," mumbled Siggy.

He was attempting to say, 'Here I am,' but his tongue became tied too.

Round and round Alf wandered, bumping into his own image and feeling more and more lost.

"Kew!" said a cat at his feet. It looked like a stray that had wandered in off the street. It was huge and had a white star on its forehead.

"Oh, what a big puddmmm mm m," mmmed Alf, his tongue finally succumbing to the spell.

"Kew! Kewmmm, mmm, mm, m," said the cat, its tongue also stilled by the magic.

"Mmm! MMM!" repeated Alf.

Then there was silence.

All their voices, Siggy, Alf and cat, were caught up and tangled by the spell.

Time passed. No one else entered the Hall. Alf and elf and cat wandered round and round and got nowhere.

"Anyone in there?" called the beer belly an hour later.

Silence.

He closed the door and locked it. He hitched the Hall of Mirrors to his truck, and drove away.

Alf's parents looked everywhere.

"Where is the little brat?" said his dad, and his mum shook her head.

"Alfreeeed!"

"Alfi!"

"Al!"

"Fred!"

"Freddy!"

"Smoochkins!"

But they called in vain.

The town square emptied. The last of the carnival packed up and left. At two in the morning only a stay dog rifled in the garbage bins in search of food. Finally Alf's parents shrugged their shoulders.

"It's getting late," yawned his mum.

"I'm tired too," said his dad.

So they went home to bed.

2 – Cam

Alf opened his eyes. He saw himself stretching to infinity in all directions. He jerked backwards in surprise and hit his head against the wall. That woke him up properly. He was still in the Hall of Mirrors, lying on the floor. It vibrated and bounced. They were on a road. It'd been hours. Light dimly filtered through two dirty skylights. He tried to speak, but his tongue wouldn't move. His voice box was dumb.

"This is a problem," he thought.

A thousand cats came walking towards him. Alf's eyes widened. The cats were huge! He tried to get away, but one of the cats rubbed against him. Alf sighed with relief—he'd forgotten about the cat. At least it was real. The cat climbed into his lap and Alf stroked it for comfort. They sat for a while. Finally the Hall of Mirrors slowed down, went over rough ground, and stopped. A truck door slammed. Then nothing.

Siggy rolled down the passageway. He had turned brown and was completely tied in a ballish tangle. He'd been desperately trying to undo his magic—but the more he struggled the more he became entangled. Luckily his limbs were flexible. If he'd had bones they'd be well and truly broken. He bumped against Alf and the cat.

Alf stared at him. "What did you do?" his eyes shouted.

Siggy looked guilty. He tried to blush but didn't succeed. He knew there was only one way out of this predicament, but he didn't want to do it.

Hours passed.

The door opened and the beer belly came in. His greasy t-shirt shouted, Cam: US Marine, in bold, army letters. He froze when he saw Alf and the cat. He didn't see Siggy. He had no second sight.

"What the fmm mum mimmm?" he said.

Cam looked puzzled. He couldn't work out what was wrong with his voice.

Alf glared at Siggy, but Siggy just shrugged.

Cam tried to get out of the Hall of Mirrors. He searched for the door, but it couldn't be found. Round and round the Hall he went. He became more and more frantic. He didn't know what was happening. All he wanted to do was to get away.

"Mmm, mmm, mm m!" he mumbled, then fell dumb completely.

At last he came back, sweating and frightened, and stood by Alf. Alf kicked Siggy. Hard. Siggy rolled down the passage, bounced off the end wall and slowly rolled back. The trailer, apparently, was on a slope. Cam wondered why the boy had kicked at thin air and what he was glaring at so intently.

Alf kicked Siggy again. Siggy's eyes pleaded, but Alf ignored him.

"Fine," thought Siggy. "Have it your way," though, truth be told, there was no other way out.

Siggy swallowed hard and let go his magic.

"Waaa!" bawled a baby beside Alf.

Cam scurried backwards in shock and Alf tried to leap to his feet but fell over. The cat hissed and darted away.

"Waaa!" the baby bawled again.

Cam and Alf stared. They were completely, utterly nonplussed.

"How did he get here?" asked Cam.

"I have no idea," said Alf.

"Waaa!" wailed the baby again, flailing his arms. He was completely naked.

Alf gingerly picked the baby up and gazed into its dark eyes. Then he saw clearly—Siggy was inside.

"I don't believe ... !" gasped Alf.

"Don't believe what?" asked Cam.

"Nothing," said Alf. "Here, take the baby," and he shoved it towards Cam.

Cam backed up. "No way," he said. "He's yours—or nobody's." This was all too strange.

The baby cried again. He was obviously hungry.

"I'm hungry too," said Alf. "Have you got anything to eat?"

"I suppose," said Cam, and he led the way out of the Hall into the bright sunshine.

Behind them followed the cat.

3 – Cam's Mum

"Oooo! What a dear," coo'd Cam's mum, immediately taking the baby from Alf. She was huger than Cam but they looked alike, even the stubble. "What's his name?"

"Donno," said Cam. "He was in the Hall of Mirrors with this lad, and he ain't seen him neither till we both did."

She gave Cam a look. "You're blubbering. He can't just appear out of nowhere like some sort of magic, now can he?"

Cam scratched his balding head.

Cam's mum turned her attention back to the baby.

"Ooo-eee! Look at his ears. They're pointy!"

Cam leaned over and looked. His brows knit together when he saw the ears.

"Well, that's not your fault, now is it?" coo'd Cam's mum, rocking the baby back and forth by her massive breasts. "And what's your name?" she said, turning to Alf.

"Alf."

"Where ya from?"

"Mainsfield."

"Mainsfield!"

Alf nodded.

"That's hundreds of miles away!"

"I suppose," said Alf. He didn't know where he was.

"Kew! Kew!" said the cat at Alf's feet. Alf pick her up.

"He's huge," said Cam's mum. "Bigger than a coon cat—and what a strange meow."

"It's a she," said Alf. "I'm calling her Kitty-o."

Cam's mum wrapped the baby in a flannel blanket and made Alf breakfast: sausages, eggs and fried bread. She gave the cat sausages and eggs too. She fed the baby from a lamb's bottle. He gulped the milk down but kept fussing. Cam's mum put a greasy finger in his mouth to sooth him.

"Ow!" she cried, jerking her hand back. "He bit me!"

They looked at the baby. The baby smiled. He had a full set of teeth.

The Darkling Beasts

"Would you look at that," said Cam's mum. "Teeth already! That's unusual. He only looks new born."

Cam shrugged. He didn't know about babies. Alf gave the baby a dirty look.

"Well, he is odd," said Cam's mum, holding him away from her. "That's for sure." She wrapped her flabby arms around him and pinched his cheek. "But he's sooooo cute!" she cooed. "You're odd, and cutesy, cutesy, cutesy, you pretty little cocky-coo!"

The baby stared at the woman in horror. Alf grinned and had to turn away to stop himself from laughing.

"Well, now," said Cam's mum, "I suppose y'all better stay. You can sleep on the sofa," she said to Alf. "Now go play."

4 – Cam's Mum's Place

Alf wandered about the property. It was in the countryside with not a neighbor in sight. It looked like a junk yard, with old cars, vans and carnival trucks scattered randomly about. There was a chicken house, and hens wandered the yard or perched on bonnets, trunks, roofs and side mirrors. An open pole barn housed some old farm equipment and two carnival trailers. A couple of sheep and three spring lambs were grazing beside the long driveway. Cam and his mum lived in a converted carnival trailer. It used to belong to 'Matilda the Wor—'; the rest of the name had been removed to insert a window. The only saving graces were the woods surrounding the property and the abundant silence. Alf found Cam's beer belly under the truck.

"What are you doing?" asked Alf.

"Changin' the oil. Pass the wrench—seven-eights."

Alf found the wrench and gave it to him.

"Thanks," said Cam.

"There's nothing to do," said Alf.

"There's lots," said Cam, sticking his head out. "Go clean the Hall mirrors. Gear's in the closet by the door. When you're done, come and find me."

Alf made a face. This isn't what he meant by needing something to do, but he went anyway. He found the cleaning gear and wandered through the Hall wiping the mirrors down. He felt a lingering fear of getting trapped again. At last he came to the exit door. It had a sign, 'You made it!' in faded, chipped paint. Alf tried the handle. The door was locked.

He went back through the maze, but found a passage he'd missed. The glass was streaked and smudged by sticky hands—ice cream by the looks of it. He cleaned the glass, working his way down the passage. At the end he turned right into a short passage. He cleaned it, and turned right into another short passage. Then he turned right again and kept cleaning. He turned right once more. Alf stopped. Ahead of him was a passage, about eight feet long, with a door at the end. A sign said: 'DON'T'.

"That's odd," thought Alf.

He looked back the way he'd come. He retraced his steps, then came back. It didn't work, it couldn't be right: turn right into a short passage, then again, then again; then the next passage should be either very short or not there at all—definitely not a long passage. It didn't make sense. He walked to the door and stared at the sign. It was old, but the letters were bold: 'DON'T'.

"Alf! Alf! What's keeping you?" shouted Cam. "Come here!"

Alf went to the entrance.

"How long does it take to clean a few mirrors?" asked Cam, eyeing him.

Alf shrugged and tried not to look at Cam's breasts or his hairy chest sticking out of his tight t-shirt.

"Go clean the truck cab. It's filthy."

It was. There were food wrappers, soda cans, popcorn, chips, candy wrappers and bread crumbs. Alf found two moldy sandwiches. He dumped everything into a plastic bag and wiped the dash and seats with a cloth. He was getting hungry.

"Good job, lad," said Cam, peering inside. "Looks like new."

* * *

Cam's mum served fried canned meat on slices of fried bread for lunch. It was greasy. The baby fussed the whole time. Finally Cam's mum gave him a crust to chew.

"He can't be teething," she said. "He's already got a full set. And I'd swear he's grown since breakfast."

Alf stopped eating. He stared.

The baby was bigger.

Cam eyed the baby too. "Oh, aye, he's bigger, for sure." He reached over and poked the baby's tummy. "And he's getting fat," he chuckled. "This one's a right pig. Snort-snort. He's singular."

The baby turned red, then sneezed loudly—achoo! Snot shot out of his nose.

Cam's mum laughed. "He is singular, isn't he," she agreed, wiping the baby's nose with a used paper towel. "A singular little elf baby, aren't ya my sweetykins."

"We can call him Marmaduke," said Alf. "Marmaduke Snotty."

The baby kicked and tried to stand up. He looked angry and his face turned purple. Cam's mum pushed him back into the cardboard box she'd lined with a blanket.

"That ain't a nice name," she said, giving him a greasy kiss on the mouth. "He's teasing you, isn't he coochy-coo? Alf's teasing you, Alf's teasing you. He's a bad, bad boy, munchy, munchy, munchy," and Cam's mum tickled the baby's tummy until he looked like he'd burst.

Alf chuckled.

5 – Gopher Throw

"Come on! Get up!" said Cam, mussing Alf's hair. "We have to get ready."

"For what?" said Alf, stretching.

"For work. For payin' Bill," said Cam, going outside. "We're on the road again tomorrow."

Alf didn't want to get up. The baby had fussed all night. It kept waking him up. Cam's mum had put him into a laundry basket and left him in the living room along with Alf.

The baby started crying again.

"Waaa! Waaa! Waaa!"

"Shush!" hissed Alf. "Enough!"

"I'm hungry," said the baby.

"What?" said Alf, sitting up and peering into the laundry basket.

"I'm hungry. Feed me and I'll shut up. It's horrible being this small."

Alf stared at the baby. It was definitely Siggy, but he couldn't get his head around it. The baby had grown overnight—and he was speaking.

"Waaa! Waaa! Waaa!" cried the baby.

"Siggy! Stop it!"

"Only if you feed me."

"I can't cook," whispered Alf. "Besides, I don't know how to look after babies."

"Waaa! Waaa!" wailed the baby.

"Siggy!"

Just then Cam's mum walked in. She eyed Alf.

"Were you two talking?"

"No," said Alf.

"Sounded like it," she said as she picked the baby up. "By God, he's big. Look at the size of him. He's grown three inches!"

"Waaa!" wailed the baby. "Waaa! Waaa! Waaa!"

"Oh, you're hungry, I know you are, sweetie boo-boos," said Cam's mum, holding the baby over her shoulder and thumping his back. "Let mama get you some foody-woodies."

The baby winked at Alf, then turned towards her fleshy ear. "Waaa! Waaa!" he screamed at full volume, and off Cam's mum rushed to make him breakfast.

Alf and Cam spent the morning repainting the gopher throw trailer. The outside had a pathetic mural showing a set of hills and gophers sticking their heads out of their burrows. Most of it had been scratched, scraped and rubbed. The new colors didn't match very well, sometimes not at all.

"Never mind," said Cam, belching from his gassy beer. "No one notices at night. Adds to the charm, I say."

The back of the trailer opened up. Gophers popped randomly out of their holes and customers threw balls at them. It looked easy, until you tried. The timing of the gophers popping up and down was a fraction less than the time it took to see a gopher and throw. If you did hit one you got a stuffed gopher as a prize. If you hit three in a row you got the huge stuffed gopher sitting in the corner. It looked really old.

"Who drives this rig?" asked Alf.

"Me mum."

"Where's all the other carnival folks," asked Alf. He hadn't seen a soul.

"Here, there, everywhere," said Cam. "We don't live together—least ways not all of us. God forbid. We're an odd enough assortment as is. We just meet up, set up, split up. Then onto the next town, wherever and whenever that is. Bill's the owner. Like I said earlier, Bill's got to be paid."

Cam chuckled at his lame joke.

"Is this all you do?" asked Alf.

"Course not," said Cam. "I exterminate rats and stuff—when I can get the work and we're not on the road; mostly in winter."

"Lunch," screeched Cam's mum from the trailer. She didn't even bother to open the door.

They went into the kitchen. The baby was sitting in a high chair with a tray. In front of him was a bowl of mush and he was eating it with a spoon.

Cam frowned. "He sits," he said.

Alf stared too. It was a little eerie. One day ago he was newborn.

"He does nothing but eat, eat, eat," said Cam's mum. "Breakfast, snack, elevenses, snack and now lunch. He'll eat us out of house and home."

"Where'd you get the high chair?" asked Cam.

"Out in the shed. It was yours."

They sat down to eat: fried canned meat on fried bread. The baby finished his bowl. He threw it on the floor and demanded meat and fried bread too. Soon he was smacking his lips and making a greasy mess. Afterwards he crunched on carrots.

"He's uncanny, that one," said Cam, leaning back in his chair and resting his hands on his round belly.

The baby grinned and looked at him, his sharp teeth gleaming.

6—Two Cats

Alf went to the Hall of Mirrors after lunch. It was locked. He heard the cat meowing inside. He went around to the exit door on the off chance. It was still locked.

"Cam, the cat's in the Hall of Mirrors," said Alf.

Cam was grinding a piece of metal in the tool shed. Sparks were flying everywhere. He stopped working and looked at Alf.

"Couldn't be," he said.

"Why not?"

"The cat's with me mum."

Alf frowned. He turned on his heel and went to the house. Cam's mum looked up as he opened the door.

"Where's Kitty-o?" he asked.

The cat appeared from the bedroom. She saw Alf and ran past him out the door. She stopped and looked back, her long tail swishing in the air. She mewed, then headed for the Hall of Mirrors.

Alf followed. Kitty-o stopped by the entrance and mewed again. An answering cry came from inside. Alf went back to the tool shed.

"Cam, there's another cat in the Hall."

Cam stopped filing the metal and they walked over to the Hall. Kitty-o was still there. Cam put his ear to the door.

"There *is* a cat," he said, taking a bunch of keys out of his pocket.

When he opened the door another huge cat stood there. It didn't have a star on its forehead, nor a tail. It walked out the doorway with measured dignity. Cam picked it up and looked.

"It's a he. How'd he get in there?"

Cam stood for a moment, listening at the doorway. It was quiet. He turned to leave.

"Let me look in the Hall," said Alf. "Maybe there's another," but Cam shook his head and shut the door.

"Well, well, well—another coon cat," said Cam's mum when she saw the two together. "Aren't they a pretty pair." She bent over and stroked the new cat. He purred. "And friendly too," she added. "We'll call him Stumpy."

A spoon came flying across the kitchen and slammed against the wall.

"Stop that, you gremlin!" shouted Cam's mum. "That's the third time."

The baby giggled. He was trying to stand up, but kept falling on his behind. He crawled over to the two cats.

"Cats," he said, patting them. "Two cats."

"Look, Mum, he can speak and count," said Cam. "He's quick!"

"He can do a lot of things you never did," said Cam's mum sourly. "I'm going to the store to stock up for the trip and buy baby clothes. Cam, you keep fixing stuff. Alf, you stay here and mind the baby. Feed him whenever he wants and he won't be too bad. Lucky he ain't picky."

"But ... " said Alf.

"No buts. I'm going. Just do it."

7 – Siggy Stands

Alf sat in the kitchen watching Siggy crawl around. Every now and then he'd stop and try to stand up.

"What are you trying to do?" asked Alf.

"Stand up, you idiot. Can't you see? It's hard. I had no idea humans had to work so hard just to walk around."

Alf shrugged. He couldn't remember learning to walk. "What's going to happen?" he asked. "Better yet, what is happening? Why did you change into a baby?"

"My magic tied us up in the Hall," said Siggy. "It was confused by the mirrors. I had to let my magic go or we'd be stuck in there forever."

"So you have no magic left?"

"None," said Siggy. "It's all tied up in making my body, and here I am, growing. I'm always hungry too. It's awful to be hungry. Give me something to eat."

Alf looked in the fridge and took out a yoghurt. Siggy tried to grab it.

"No," said Alf. "I'll feed you—otherwise there'll be a mess and I'll have to clean it up."

Alf found a spoon and fed Siggy as he sat on the floor.

"Yum," said Siggy, gulping it down. "What's that taste?"

Alf showed him the jar.

"I can't read yet, you ding-dong," said Siggy, pushing it away.

"Maple syrup," said Alf. "And there's something else. I thought Kitty-o was a stray, but she isn't. The other cat appeared in the Hall of Mirrors—but it was locked."

Siggy stopped eating.

"And I found a passageway in the Hall. It went right and right and right and that should have been the end, but it wasn't. There's another passage, a long one with a door. It has a sign that says 'DON'T' in big letters."

Siggy stared at Alf. Then he stood up. His eyes were round with effort. He teetered back and forth on his tiny feet. "A door," he said, and fell backwards, hitting his head.

"Waaa! Waaa! Waaa!" cried Siggy.

Cam came rushing in from outside.

"What did you do?" he demanded, looking at Alf.

"Nothing," said Alf. "He was trying to stand up and fell over."

"Waaa! Waaa! Waaa!" wailed Siggy.

"You've gotta hold him," said Cam. "Everyone's gotta learn easy like. Here, like this," and he lifted Siggy up and held him under the arms. Siggy stopped crying and teetered forwards with his support.

"See," said Cam. "Do that."

"I'm calling him Siggy," said Alf, taking over from Cam. "That's his name."

"Fine by me," said Cam, going back outside. "Call him what you want."

8 – *Perkiomenville*

The next day Alf got up early and went outside. Kitty-o and Stumpy followed. He went over to the Hall and tried the door. Cam had not locked it after letting Stumpy out. He went inside, the cats at his heels. Round and round he went until he came to the door. It still said,

The Darkling Beasts

'DON'T'. He touched the handle and the door swung open. Ahead lay a silver passage. The cats ran through and turned a corner. Outside, the house door slammed open.

"Alf—breakfast!" yelled Cam's mum.

Alf stepped back and the door swung to. He slipped out of the Hall and back into the kitchen.

"Where have you been?" asked Cam's mum.

Cam was already up and sitting at the table. He stared at Alf.

Before he could answer Siggy toddled into the kitchen all by himself.

"Me hungry," he declared, grinning broadly at everyone. He'd grown three more inches overnight.

"Great," said Cam. "Now get yourself out of diapers, you stink."

Soon they headed out in convoy, Cam's mum leading in the gopher throw truck. They stopped in Upper Farnon to buy larger clothes and a car seat at the secondhand store for Siggy. Then they joined the freeway.

Alf traveled with Cam. The truck shook badly. It got worse the faster they went.

"Why does it shake so much?" asked Alf.

"Tires," said Cam. "We need new ones. Hope these don't blow. Last time I almost crashed. Missed the tree by a foot."

They headed south towards Perkiomenville, stopping every hour to feed Siggy.

"It'll take all day," groaned Cam, but there was nothing he could do about it.

They rolled into town late. The square was already crowded with trucks, booths and tents. Cam and his mum had a tough time maneuvering into place.

"Where you been?" men shouted. "Sleeping in? Drinking's more like it."

A man in an over-styled suit walked up. "At least you're here," he snarked in a half friendly manner.

"What's the rush, Bill," said Cam. "We don't open till tomorrow."

"Ordinance," said Bill. "No work or noise past ten. You have half an hour."

Cam's mum came over with Siggy and put him in Alf's arms. "Here, you mind him," she said. "Don't let him get run over."

Siggy was heavy. Alf put him down and held his hand. They wandered about watching people work. They were putting the finishing touches to the stalls, stringing lights, hanging stuffed ducks, raising canopies and attaching ropes. They worked quickly and efficiently. They'd done this a thousand times before. Nobody paid Alf and Siggy much attention, except for one woman with stiff hair. She came up and stared at Siggy. She smiled.

"Aren't you a cutie," she said. "You're so small and you're walking already. You look like an elf," and she bent over and pinched his chubby cheek.

"That's because I am, you moron," said Siggy, giving her an evil grin.

The woman's smile vanished. She stood up. Her gaze flashed back and forth uncertainly between Siggy and Alf. Then she walked off.

"Stop it," said Alf.

"I hate it when they treat me like a fool," said Siggy. "All sugary sweet and coochy-coo-coo and saying things as if I don't understand. Besides, what's wrong with looking like an elf? I am!"

"Not any more," said Alf. "Haven't you noticed? You're one of us now. And you're bald."

Siggy touched his head. It was still covered with baby fuzz.

"I'll grow hair by tomorrow," said Siggy. "Then I'll look more like an elf."

"But you're not," said Alf.

"I am so," said Siggy.

"Do magic then," said Alf.

Siggy twisted his mouth.

"See," said Alf.

"I'm *not* human," said Siggy defiantly, toddling off on his new legs and trying to keep his balance on the rough ground.

Alf wondered why his back was hunched.

When they got back to the Hall of Mirrors Cam was not around. Alf tried the door. It was locked.

"I opened the 'DON'T' door," said Alf.

"What was there?" asked Siggy.

The Darkling Beasts

"A silver passage."

"I'd be careful," said Siggy.

"Kew!" mewed a cat from inside the Hall. "Kew!"

Alf and Siggy looked at each other. Just then Cam's mum walked up. "There you are. Time for bed, you two."

"There's a cat in there," said Alf, pointing.

"Kew!" said the cat.

"Couldn't be," said Cam's mum. "We didn't bring them."

She fished around in her purse and found the key. She opened the door and out came the cat.

"Kitty-o!" cried Alf, picking her up.

"Kitty-o! Kitty-o! Kitty-o!" shouted Siggy, reaching up and stroking her fur.

"She must have slipped inside before we left," said Cam's mum. "Either that or there's a hole in the trailer." She looked at the cat. "Well, she can't stay at the hotel." She took her from Alf and tossed her back into the Hall.

"Kitty," called Siggy, distressed.

Alf reached for the door as it swung shut, but he was too late. It clicked firmly. Cam's mum locked it.

"Can't she come?" asked Alf.

Cam's mum shook her head. "She'll look after herself. It's late—let's go," and she scooped up Siggy and marched off.

9 – *Hotel Ritz*

They spent the night in Hotel Ritz. It was cheap and the room stank of stale cigarette smoke. The metal ashtrays were nailed to the night stands beside the two beds. A sign over the TV said, 'NO SMOKING'.

Alf tried the TV and got nothing but hissing and static. Cam hit the side and it stopped working altogether.

"Brain rot! That's what those are," said Cam's mum. "Better off without them, I say."

Alf and Siggy slept on the floor. They were both in their clothes. Cam's mum had gotten Siggy some pj's but he refused to get undressed.

They could hear people fighting downstairs. The hotel's neon sign glared brightly through the thin curtains. It flickered and kept Alf awake. At last he drifted off into sleep.

He woke to Siggy shaking him.

"What?" said Alf.

"I'm hungry."

Alf rolled over.

Siggy shook him again. "Alf! I'm hungry."

Alf sat up. "What time is it?"

"Two-ten," said Siggy, pointing to the clock.

Alf looked at Siggy. "You can read?" he said.

"Well, duh."

"You couldn't a day ago."

"That was a day ago. I have to eat."

"For God's sake," said Alf, "wait till breakfast."

"I can't," said Siggy. "It's killing me. How hungry would you be if you were growing three inches a night?"

Alf saw his point. He got up and snuck around the room. Nothing. Cam was snoring and his mum blubbered. He looked in Cam's mum's purse. He found cherry chewing gum and gave it to Siggy.

"This is totally non-nutritional," said Siggy, looking at the label. He opened the gum wrappers and stuffed the lot into his mouth anyway.

Alf rummaged in the purse some more. He found the key to the Hall of Mirrors in a side pocket. He hesitated, then kept it.

"This isn't enough," said Siggy.

"That's all there is," shrugged Alf.

"Fine," said Siggy. "Lie down and close your ears."

Alf lay down and covered his ears.

"Waaa! Waaa! Waaa!" wailed Siggy. "Me hungry! Waaa! Waaa! Waaa!"

"Oh, mercy," shouted Cam, sitting up. "Feed the brat!"

Cam's mum got out of bed. She searched her stuff but found nothing.

"I've got to get him something," she mumbled.

"Waaa! Waaa! Waaa!" wailed Siggy in his most demanding voice.

The Darkling Beasts

Someone thumped the wall from next door. "Keep the brat quiet!" they yelled.

Cam's mum sighed. She put on her overcoat. "Come on," she said, picking Siggy up.

Alf jumped up too. He slipped on his shoes and followed. The hotel clerk stared as they walked through the foyer.

"He's hungry," said Cam's mum, pointing her thumb at Siggy.

"To the right," said the clerk. "Two blocks. Can't miss it."

They walked out into the night. The odd car swooshed past. Some prowled down the street, music pumping from inside. Others were silent, their windows tinted and dark. A black cat slinked around a garbage bin, staring at them. They passed a couple of women wearing sparkly clothes and high heels. Alf looked at them. The women give him a half grin.

"Why are they so sad?" asked Alf.

"Life," said Cam's mum.

Siggy stared at them. "That's not life," he said. "They're starving."

On the second block they found an all-night store. It didn't have much to eat. They bought popcorn and a synthetic wiener on a bun. Siggy wolfed them down. Then he drank orange and apple juice.

"More," he said.

Cam's mum bought ginger ale and bags of peanuts. Siggy liked the peanuts and shelled them as they walked back to the hotel. Alf looked down at him. He had grown and his clothes were tight. He toddled confidently. Alf wondered when he'd stop growing. The night ladies were gone.

10 – *Alf the Barker*

Siggy had hair in the morning. Bright red hair. Very bright. His baby fluff was gone and a silky mop three inches long sat on his head. Everyone stared. It was quite the sight. Siggy seemed pleased and gave Alf a toothy grin as he ate a huge breakfast. They were sitting in a Chinese restaurant with tired plastic seats. Siggy ate eggs, eggs and more eggs. Alf swore he'd grown another inch since last night's expedition.

"Protein!!!" shouted Siggy excitedly.

Cam stared at him. "He's a stopper, isn't he?" he said, and patted him on the back. "Hey, what's that lump?" he asked.

Siggy twisted away. "Nothing—M-Y-O-B."

"Fine," said Cam, and he turned to his mum. "You'll have to get him another set of clothes—and shoes. Get a bunch at the thrift store just to be sure." He paused. "Kids don't normally grow so quick, do they Mum?"

Cam's mum tossed her eyes upwards and belched.

"I'll take Alf," said Cam. "He can look after the Hall till you get back. There's never much happening first thing anyway."

Cam's mum slurped her tea. She nodded. She looked tired.

"You have to bring Kitty-o something to eat," said Alf, and Cam's mum nodded again without saying anything.

"The cats are at home," said Cam.

"Not Kitty-o," said Cam's mum. "There must be a hole in the trailer."

When Alf and Cam got to the Hall of Mirrors Cam unlocked the door.

"Here, kitty, kitty," called Cam.

"Here Kitty-o," called Alf.

There was no reply.

Cam lowered the metal steps leading up to the door. He went in, followed by Alf. They wandered the passageways. Nothing. No cat—nor the passage that Alf had seen before.

"That's strange," said Cam. "You sure she was here?"

Alf nodded. And it was strange. He couldn't work it out.

Cam shrugged. "Must be a hole somewhere. I better find it. Cats are fine, but we don't want rats in here."

Cam led Alf back out. He slid a metal table from underneath the Hall trailer, and set it up beside the steps.

"It's easy," said Cam. "Dollar a shot. Give them change and point the way. If anything goes wrong, shout. I'm just across the aisle."

Alf sat at the table. It had a cash tray bolted underneath on one side. That held the seed money. Beside it was a drop slot for extra money that wouldn't be needed. The money fell into a metal box welded to the tabletop. The tabletop, in turn, had a thick metal chain running to the trailer. No one was going to steal their cash in a hurry.

Alf waited. At first it was fun. He watched people pass and smiled at them. But no one bought a ticket. He became bored and slouched in his chair. It was morning and there wasn't much activity, though some school kids were showing up.

"Sit up, Alf," called Cam from across the aisle. "Look lively. No one wants to come to a dead fish."

Alf sat up and tried to look interested. After a while he stood to ease his butt. By now everyone seemed to have customers except for him. He sat down again. It was twelve o'clock and still no one had shown the slightest interest in the Hall.

"Call your wares," said Cam. "That sometimes works."

Alf made a sour face.

"Go on," said Cam. "Try it. Be a barker."

"Hall of Mirrors," called Alf weakly.

A passerby sniggered, and his girlfriend elbowed him in the ribs.

"Don't mind Jo Public," said Cam. "Who do they think they are anyway?"

Alf dug deep. He stood beside the stairs.

"Hall of Mirrors!" he cried at the top of his lungs. "Come and see the Marvelous, Magical, Mysterious, Hall of Mirrors! Guaranteed to Amaze!"

Cam and the surrounding stall owners burst out laughing. Then they cheered and clapped. Three ran over, dropped a dollar into the till, and scooted through the Hall in a flash.

"See," said Cam, spreading his arms. "The money just flows in!"

"Hall of Mirrors!" cried Alf again, grabbing a passerby by the sleeve. "Come and see the Marvelous, Magical, Mysterious, Hall of Mirrors! Guaranteed to Amaze!"

The passerby grinned, threw a dollar onto the table and entered the Hall. Alf put the money away and waited for the man to exit. The exit door was at the rear of the trailer. It had steps like the entrance, but also a railing that guided the customers back into the main thoroughfare. Alf waited. The man did not come out. He waited some more, and still he didn't appear.

"Cam," called Alf after twenty minutes. "Come here."

Cam came over.

"Remember the man that went in?"

Cam nodded.

"He hasn't come out."

"What?" said Cam. "The one from ages ago?"

Alf nodded.

Cam went inside. A minute later he came out the exit. He looked at Alf and cocked his head. "You sure?"

Alf nodded again. Cam could see that he was worried.

"You must be mistaken," said Cam. "There's no one there."

11 – Doyen of Fashion

Siggy and Cam's mum came back. Siggy was dressed in blue jeans, red t-shirt and bright yellow baseball cap. His hair was an inch longer.

Alf laughed. "Good one, Siggy," he said. "Very nice."

Siggy smiled. The cap pushed his pointy ears outwards and he looked entirely elfish. His dark, slanted, almond shaped eyes glinted mischievously underneath the visor. His only flaw was the slightly swollen upper back—though he walked perfectly straight.

"I am superb," he declared. "A doyen of fashion."

"A what?" said Cam from the gopher throw. "What's a bloody doyen. Sounds like a parasite."

"Listen to him," said Cam's mum. "He can read as well. Grabbed a book at the thrift store and started to read aloud—just like that. And it wasn't a kid's book neither. Now he's full of fancy words."

She put a bag of clothes into the truck cab and took her place at the gopher throw.

"Here," she said, holding out a few dollars to Alf. "Go get something to eat. Ester over there will feed you cheap. Bring me back a sandwich and soda—and one for Cam too."

Siggy grabbed the dollars from her hand and stuffed them in his pocket.

"Me buy," he said.

"Don't 'me buy' me," said Cam's mum, swatting him on the butt. "You can speak proper when you want."

29

Siggy laughed. "You are incontrovertibly correct," he said with a grin and toddled off on his tiny legs.

Cam's jaw dropped.

"That kid ... !" he said. "We'll have to buy a bloody dictionary next."

"Not that you could use it," snarked his mum.

Alf and Siggy wandered through the crowd.

"A man went into the Hall of Mirrors while you were gone," said Alf.

"So?" said Siggy.

"He didn't come out."

Siggy looked at Alf.

"What's going on?" said Alf. "I don't get it."

"It must be an interdimensional portal," said Siggy.

"A what?"

"A door, a portal. My magic might have activated one, or maybe it's the way the mirrors are set."

"A door to where?"

"To where it came from," said Siggy.

Alf was quiet for a moment. "A door to where you came from?"

Siggy shrugged uncertainly. It was odd seeing someone so small thinking so intently. "I doubt it," he said at last. "My world borders yours, but there are lots of other places, different worlds, more than you know. Some are good, others bad. Some are just ... different."

"Different?"

Siggy pulled at his cap. "Different," he said. "That's all." He was struggling. "So different that you can't say it's like this or like that or like anything you can think or know."

"What happens if you go to one of those places?" asked Alf.

"You're lost," said Siggy, a shadow passing over his face.

They came to Ester's Eatery. She made sandwiches, salads, hearty soups and grilled genuine, homemade German bratwurst on toasted, sprouted whole grain buns. She was always busy. She made good food because the carnival folk relied on her—if she didn't they'd spend days without something decent to eat. Joe Public didn't eat there much, they weren't looking for a proper meal at a carnival.

"So you're the strangely strange twins everyone's talking about," said Ester by way of greeting. She tugged on Siggy's cap. "You do look like a pixie."

Alf half expected Siggy to do something unexpected. He did. He gave her a huge smile and a hug.

Ester chucked and hugged him back. "So what you want, my luvs?"

"A bratwurst," said Alf. The smell was delicious.

"With everything!" said Siggy enthusiastically.

"Right you are, little man," said Ester.

"I'm not a man," said Siggy. "I'm an elf."

"True," said Ester. "But don't go advertising it. No one believes in them anyway."

They sat at a table behind the stall. It was reserved for the carnival folk. It had a checkered tablecloth, folding chairs and napkins. A sign on the table said: YOUR MOM IS NOT HERE. CLEAN UP AFTER YOURSELF—PROPERLY—OR DON'T COME BACK. The table was spotless.

It was past midday and the sun was bright. They sat looking around.

"There," said Ester, putting down a big spread. "How's that?"

"Thanks," said Siggy. "It looks salubrious."

Ester gave Siggy an eye. "And what does Cam and his mum want?"

"Sandwiches and soda," said Alf.

Siggy and Alf ate their fill. They put their paper plates in the trash and wiped the table carefully. Siggy handed her the money.

"I don't want it," said Ester, handing it back.

"How do you work that out?" asked Siggy.

"I do what I like," said Ester, and she handed him a chocolate bar.

Siggy's eyes widened.

"Share it with your brother," she said, nodding at Alf.

12 – The Man

That night Alf woke Siggy.

"I'm going," he said.

Siggy wavered.

"Come on," Alf whispered. "Let's go see."

They pulled on their clothes and silently crept out of the room. The desk clerk had his head on his arm and they snuck past. It was late, three in the morning, and no one was around. They went to the town square and made their way through the deserted and shuttered stalls. They stopped at the Hall of Mirrors and Alf put the key in the door. It was dark inside and they switched on the lights. The lights were long rows of LEDs running along the ceiling of each isle. Instantly Alf and Siggy saw themselves stretching into the distances everywhere among the stars. They walked the maze, checking all the side passages.

"It's here," said Alf, catching his breath.

Siggy looked down the passage. It seemed like any other. They walked down, turned right, right again and quickly right again. There was the long passage stretching before them. At the end was the door. The sign said 'DON'T'.

They went to the door and stood in front of it. Alf reached out and touched the handle. The door opened. The silver passage was lined with a seamless, mirror-like surface that covered the floor, walls and ceiling. At the end it curved softly to the left and slightly upwards. Suddenly a man appeared from around the corner, running. He was frantic. He halted when he saw Alf and Siggy, then burst past them and ran into the Hall. He stopped and looked back. Alf recognized him. It was the man who had gone in earlier. For a moment the man peered down the silvery passageway. His eyes widened in terror. He turned and fled the Hall of Mirrors, crashing heavily into the walls as he went. Alf and Siggy followed. They watched as he staggered away into the night, looking about in a daze.

"Kew!" said a cat.

"Kew!" said another.

It was Kitty-o and Stumpy. Alf picked Kitty-o up and they went back to the door. It was still wide open. 'DON'T' the sign said, but they did.

13 – Other Place

Alf and Siggy were on a hill. Behind them was a hollow tree. It was like a baobab tree, with a massive, swollen trunk, and above, root-like branches poorly dressed with leaves. A giant tear in the trunk made a rough doorway. That's where they'd come out. As soon as they were outside Kitty-o struggled free of Alf's arms and flew away with Stumpy.

"Hey!" cried Alf and Siggy in surprise as they watched their sinuous bodies take to the air. Their wings were covered with soft down and had an odd, lemniscatory stroke—like the wings of a stingray moving through water.

They were on a rise overlooking what seemed to be a city; a garden city with forest covering the ground, but with tall, thin, earthen-colored spires rising into the sky. The spires were scattered randomly: in groups, alone, in pairs, on hills, in valleys, in rows. They stretched to the horizon. Alf counted over a hundred.

"Where are we?" asked Alf.

"I'm not sure," said Siggy, frowning. "We'll have to see."

"What do you mean?" asked Alf.

"Sometimes it takes a while to really know where you are," said Siggy.

Alf looked at the sky. An orange sun was directly overhead. The sky was a milky blue. As Alf gazed upward an overwhelming urge took hold of him, as if the sky was drawing him into itself through the power of longing.

"Alf," cried Siggy, roughly yanking on his arm. "Don't."

Alf came back to himself with a shock. Only when he began to breathe again did he realize that he'd stopped breathing altogether.

'Keeee kee-reee! Keeee kee-reee!' sang a songbird, flying through the trees. It was yellow and red. It flew incredibly fast.

'Keeee kee-reee! Keeee kee-reee!' sang another, and another, following the first. Their calls could be heard for a long time.

"Let's go back," said Siggy.

Alf looked at him. "Why? This looks fine."

Siggy seemed anxious, but Alf didn't see it, he wanted to explore.

"Let's check out those buildings," he said, and started waking.

Siggy tagged behind dutifully as they made their way through the forest and came to a well-worn path free of leaf litter. They followed it. Other paths and tracks occasionally crisscrossed it here and there, but no one was seen. The trees were all in leaf. Some had bright flowers high in the canopy—scarlet, lilac and yellow. The air was warm and scented. It was humid and a breeze blew constantly, sighing quietly in the branches overhead.

After half a mile a tower loomed above them. At a distance the towers looked slim and elegant, but up close this one had a shabby feel to it. The round walls were a warm yellow-brown. They were clearly hand-made and shaped, as if mud was packed and piled up in stages. No bricks were used. On the outside of the tower a stairway spiraled up and up and up, a small landing stopping at a single doorway on each floor. The doors were staggered randomly and the stairs climbed now steeply, now less so, as if each floor had been made by a different person with a different stride and a different degree of building skill. The windows were always arched, but sized and set differently on each floor. Some were tiny and others large. None had glass.

Something rustled loudly near them in the forest, followed by a moist chomping sound. Alf and Siggy peered through the trees and stopped.

"Now that's odd," said Alf. "Definitely."

A fat beast floated across the forest floor. It looked vaguely like an octopus, with fleshy, hairless tentacles hanging towards the ground. They were reaching out and gathering forest litter and pulling it towards a central mouth hidden underneath. Above was a huge, balloon-like, oblong body, covered with a short, brown coat. It had two dark, dreamy eyes.

Alf and Siggy left the path and walked closer. It seemed harmless. It stopped eating as they approached. It became very, very still.

"I wouldn't go any closer," said a voice.

Alf and Siggy turned. A girl about Alf's age stood on the path. They hadn't heard her coming.

She was barefooted and ragged, but her face and eyes were clear and warm.

"I saw you coming," she said when they didn't say anything. "I'm from the tilting."

Alf and Siggy just looked at her.

"There," she said, pointing to the building.

"We wanted to see the building," said Alf. "We've never seen one up close."

The girl laughed. "Ha!" she shouted, not believing them.

The beast made a whooshing sound at the girl's shout. Alf and Siggy spun around and saw it floating into the air. It used its tentacles to grasp the branches and quickly move away.

"Where are you from?" asked the girl, eyeing them.

Siggy and Alf hesitated, not knowing what to say.

"We're from another … " began Alf, but Siggy kicked his leg.

"We're from the tree on the hill," said Siggy.

"The hollow one," said Alf.

"The drummer tree? At the top of the hill?"

Alf and Siggy nodded, hoping it was the right thing to say.

The girl obviously didn't believe them. She looked them up and down.

"Have it your way," she said at last. "Want to come up?"

Alf nodded yes, and Siggy nodded no. Alf grabbed Siggy's hand and pulled him after the girl as she led the way.

They quickly come to a high wall surrounding the building. Nasty spikes pointing in all directions were set on top. The girl knocked on a door within a heavy gate, also topped with spikes. A peephole opened and an eye looked out.

"It's fine," she said.

The peephole closed. Three metal bars slid across the door and it creaked open. They went in and the door slammed behind them. The three bolts scraped shut.

"This is Mama," said the girl, gesturing to an old woman.

"I'm Alf," said Alf, putting out his hand.

The old woman stared at it, then at him. She patted his hand uncertainly.

"I'm Siggy," said Siggy, not putting out his hand.

"What's your real name?" asked the old woman.

"Singular," said Siggy. "Singular Elf."

The Darkling Beasts

"Makes sense with those pointy ears," said the old woman. "Keep an eye on him," she said to the girl. "Look at those eyes. And don't be fooled by his size."

She turned her back and hobbled into a hut beside the door. She sat on a bench and ignored them.

The girl led the way towards the building. The courtyard was almost completely bare of plants; nothing but beaten earth and a few wisps of grass. Around the edge, against the defensive wall, were a number of lean-to sheds.

"I'm Mia," she said, smiling at them. "Don't mind Mama, she's sometimes a little grumpy."

"Is she really your mom?" asked Alf.

"No," said Mia. "That's just what we call her. If you're sick she looks after you."

They came to the stairs and began to climb. There was no railing and the steps were narrow, sometimes more so, sometimes less. Siggy raced ahead in a burst of energy. Alf grinned at his small legs pumping up the stairs.

"He's cute," said Mia. "So small."

"But growing," said Alf.

"That's normal," said Mia.

"Not five or six inches a day."

Mia looked at Alf strangely, but said nothing. Alf wished he'd kept his mouth shut.

"What's wrong with his back?" asked Mia.

Alf shrugged. "I don't know. It doesn't seem to bother him, but he doesn't talk about it."

They circled the building once and approached a landing.

"Hi, Vassa," Mia called out.

They passed a window on the landing. Alf glanced in. The room was almost bare, but the walls and ceiling were sculpted and shaped, which made it warm and inviting.

Alf scratched the clay. It was hard. Very hard. His fingernails left no mark at all.

"You really haven't been to one of these buildings, have you?" said Mia.

Alf shook his head.

"But there are so many tiltings," said Mia, puzzled. "Besides, where else can you live?"—but Alf looked away.

Up and up and up they went, round and round. Each time as they came to a landing Mia called out, "Hello, Jhek!" or "Hello, Baz!" After ten stories Alf began to feel uneasy. It was high and the wind blew and there was no railing. He was panting. Mia stopped.

"You really, really haven't been to a tilting?" she said, still not quite believing.

Alf shook his head and looked over the landscape. He could see further now, but the city, if that's what it was, stretched onwards over the horizon. He was tempted to look at the sky. It was hard not to see it, and harder to ignore it. He tried to think of something else.

"Where's Siggy?" asked Alf, suddenly anxious. "Siggy! Siggy!"

Siggy came racing back around the corner. He had an excited gleam in his eye.

"What's up with you?" asked Alf.

"I love being so high," said Siggy. "It's like flying. Where's your home?" he asked Mia.

"Can't miss it," she said. "At the top."

Alf groaned. They had a long way to go.

Up and up and up they climbed. Alf leaned in towards the building to make sure he didn't fall off. The steps were so narrow and uneven.

Mia followed behind patiently. Alf glanced into each room as they passed. Some had people but most seemed empty, nevertheless Mia called out before each door.

"Are they all in?" asked Alf.

"Yes, no, maybe," said Mia. "You have to call just before you get to the door. Otherwise someone might come out as you're passing and knock you off. People die that way."

Alf hadn't thought of that. "You'd better tell Siggy," he said.

Mia passed him and ran up the stairs. She was light and swift.

"Hello," cried Alf loudly just before he reached the next landing.

The door opened and a man looked out.

"What's all this running about?" he said. "Some pointy-eared brat is

37

bouncing around. I nearly knocked him off the stairs. Would have served him right," and he slammed the door.

Up and up and up Alf climbed. His knees began to tremble and his steps became uncertain. He clung to the wall which now had a handhold sculpted into the clay. Sometimes he felt dizzy. At last he reached a landing with no further stairs. The door was open. Alf entered, grateful to be inside. He must be seventy floors up.

Then he noticed it—the building was swaying in the wind like a ship at sea.

14 – Night

Alf gazed at the sky through the window. It drew him outwards. "Don't look too long," said Mia, laughing.

"It pulls me," said Alf.

Mia nodded. Then she became serious. "If you're on the stairs never look up."

Alf lowered his gaze to the horizon. He could see towers for miles.

"Don't they ever fall over?" he said.

"What?" asked Mia.

"These buildings. They're so slim."

"Sometimes," said Mia, "especially when the summer storms come. Then they bend and break."

"What about the people inside?" asked Alf.

"They go to the sky," said Mia, surprised at the question.

Alf walked to another window. The breeze through the room ruffled his hair. It was beautiful and peaceful up here, but tenuous.

"Who builds them?" he asked.

"We do ... the Instars," said Mia. "We use clay and the juice of the tilting tree. The juice makes the mud hard, yet supple. It's incredibly strong. When someone joins a tilting they make their own floor, with help or without. You just build on top of the highest person."

"Did you build this room?" asked Alf.

Mia nodded. "It took a while—though people helped. I don't think anyone will build on top of me."

"I bet that's what the person below you said," chimed in Siggy. He was exploring the room as he was too small to see out the windows. There wasn't much to see: one large round room with three windows without glass on one side. Away from the windows was a bed of coarse blankets on a raised platform. A rough wooden table was attached to the wall and around it bags hung from pegs. There was nothing on the floor. It sloped gently towards a drain hole in the wall—to let the water out when it rained, Siggy presumed. Between the bed and the table was a ladder; a single branch with steps cut into it.

"What's this for?" Siggy asked. "Does it go to the roof?"

Mia nodded and Siggy scampered up.

"Lift the hatch and push it aside," said Mia when he got to the top, but it was too heavy for him.

Mia climbed up and pushed it open. Siggy followed her outside and Alf joined them.

Alf looked around. It was dizzying and his feet felt uncertain on the swaying deck. From here he could see a broad, cultivated hill. On top of the hill was a golden pyramid. He'd been too distracted to notice it coming up the stairs.

"What's that?" he asked, pointing.

"That's Golden Hill," said Mia. "It's for the Golden Ones."

"Where?" said Siggy, coming over.

Alf pointed.

"Oh, that. I saw it coming up the stairs. Is there food there?"

"Lots," said Mia in a level voice, as if it had nothing much to do with her. "That's where all the food is grown, for us Instars and the Golden Ones as well."

Siggy swiftly swung himself down the ladder like a monkey. His eyes were gleaming. He loved it up high. "I'm hungry," he called up to Mia. "What's to eat?"

Alf and Mia came down. She opened one of the bags hanging from the wall. Inside were a few odd looking nuts.

"Is that all?" asked Siggy, disappointed.

"All for the next few days," said Mia.

"Days?" cried Siggy, a look of desperation crossing his face.

'Keeee kee-reee! Keeee kee-reee! Keeee kee-reee!' called a flock of yellow and red birds flying round and round the tower.

Siggy ran to the door to look at them, then he started down the stairs.

"Where are you going?" called Alf, but he'd already gone around the corner.

Alf sighed. "Siggy really does have to eat," he said, but Mia just looked at him.

He changed the subject. "Where are your parents?" he asked.

Mia tilted her head and looked upwards. For a moment she looked vulnerable.

They sat and waited for Siggy to return. The afternoon was getting on. The air started to cool and the sunlight reddened. Alf suddenly got up and looked out the windows. There were no long shadows. He gave Mia a puzzled look and ran up the ladder. He stuck his head out the hatch and looked up. The sun was in the same place, high in the sky, but it was smaller and had shifted from orange to red.

"The sun," he said, pointing. "The sun … " Alf couldn't work it out.

"I'd better get Siggy," said Mia, suddenly going down the stairs. "It's almost darkling."

Alf climbed onto the roof and lay down. It was the only way he could look up without feeling dizzy. The feeling wasn't unpleasant, though he felt disconnected from himself. The sun stayed in one place, but was shrinking and getting redder. From the forest came strange evening noises. Alf crawled to the low parapet and looked over. The sun made the other tiltings glow golden-red. The green canopy of the forest had darkened to a red-brown. He saw a number of large, bulbous animals float upwards to the tree tops. He stared. It was the octopus grazers. Mia had called them oaplahs. Now they were rising up, floating above the canopy, and holding onto a branch with one tentacle. They looked like dark brown, misshapen party balloons. Other life was stirring the tree tops too, but Alf was too far away to make anything out.

'Teeeee-quee-lick, teeeee-quee-lick,' sang a flock of blue birds flying past. They had a single yellow bar on each wing. They swooped left, then right, then rapidly turned and landed on the tilting. They eyed Alf half trustingly. Other birds landed on the tilting as well and began to settle down for the night.

Alf heard Mia return with Siggy just as the sun became a small point. It still hadn't moved in the sky. He climbed down.

"He was in a neighbors' room," she said, giving him a look. "Begging."

Siggy was shameless. "It was yummy," he declared, licking his lips.

Alf saw that his pockets were bulging. He didn't ask if the contents were stolen or given.

Mia handed them a blanket each and settled down on the platform. Alf expected a light to be lit, but saw no lamp or candles. Five green birds settled on her windowsill. They mourned quietly. Mia seemed to be waiting. She glanced at them from time to time in the twilight, her dark eyes gleaming. Then all light left.

A series of grunts came from the forest. They were deep and guttural. A moment later there was a wild shriek of terror and the crashing and breaking of undergrowth. This was followed by silence; then more grunting, louder and more insistent.

"What was that?" asked Alf.

"The darkling beasts," said Mia. "They come from underground. They can't get into the tiltings unless there's been a mistake."

"What happens then?" asked Siggy.

Mia's blanket rustled, as if she'd shrugged her shoulders. After a while she lay down and slept. Siggy scooted over to Alf and sat next to him. All through the night the sounds of beasts grunting, crashing, crying and screaming came from below. Alf hardly slept, and when he did he was soon woken. Finally the world lightened. The sounds instantly subsided and he fell properly asleep at last.

15 – Pyramid

The next morning they went to Golden Hill. The sun was still in the heights, slowly growing in size and shifting hue from red to orange.

"Why doesn't the sun move?" Alf asked Mia.

Mia frowned. "It never moves. It waxes towards golden yellow and wanes towards red and darkling."

"Then where does it go?"

"Away," said Mia.

Alf dropped the question.

Siggy was not interested in the sun. He had only one real interest. As they walked through the forest he kept looking for fruits and nuts. He'd grown two inches in the night and his face was pale. The lump on his back had swollen and his shirt was too tight. His bright mop needed a haircut.

"Is there nothing to eat in the forest?" he asked.

"Not really," said Mia. "There's fruit in the autumn, but in spring there's nothing. Some of the shoots are edible, but we only eat them if we're starving. There might be roots, but no one goes digging, it's too dangerous."

"Where can I dig?" asked Siggy, not worried about danger. As far as he was concerned he was in danger of dying from hunger.

"There's no use looking," said Mia. "Autumn is far away."

Alf was hungry too. It'd been a day since he'd had a good meal. The little that Mia shared didn't do much for him. They came to a clearing in the forest. The ground was torn up and a tree had been hauled down and decimated. There was blood everywhere. It was fresh; they could smell it.

"What happened here?" asked Alf.

"You heard it last night," said Mia. "I told you."

She hesitated.

"You truly don't come from here, do you?"

Siggy and Alf shook their heads. They skirted the clearing and went on. Mia walked ahead, her slim body quick and agile. Alf liked her. They walked on in silence. Other people appeared on the path or were glimpsed through the trees. More and more came until it seemed like the forest was alive with footsteps. All were headed toward the Golden Hill.

Suddenly the forest gave way and a high wall stretched into the distance on either side. It had widely spaced gates. The top of the wall was a jungle of deadly spikes. They entered a gate and instantly the land was intensely cultivated. There were crops of all kinds. Alf recognized none of the plants, but there were fields of vegetables and, presumably, grain; also orchards and pastures with fat, docile looking animals and others with wooly fleece. Farmers and gardeners were scattered about doing manual labor or hauling carts. One field had lots of people harvesting a crop. A couple of men in black clothing stood in the shade of a tree and watched them. There were no machines and no beasts of burden.

"Don't stare at the guards," said Mia when she saw Alf and Siggy looking at them.

"Guards?" said Siggy.

"You'll see," said Mia.

The pyramid loomed large on the crest of the hill. It was much bigger than it appeared from the tilting. The pyramid glittered and shone brightly in the morning light. It was simple, impressive and beautiful. Alf and Siggy forgot their hunger and stared.

As they approached they saw that the upper third was of solid gold, but the lower two-thirds had unglazed, rectangular openings at harmonic intervals. The path they were on joined another, and another, until they wove together and created a great avenue leading to a white stone staircase with a landing running around the whole building. Massive entries with three huge double doors were placed at the center of each facet of the pyramid. At each door stood a guard. They were bloated and pasty and had trouble breathing. All looked identical, like clones, and all wore black uniforms with black wraparound sunglasses. The lenses were slightly bulbous and completely opaque. The guards watched everyone who entered intently. Mia and Alf passed through easily.

"Who's that?" barked a guard, pointing at Siggy.

Mia stopped. "A friend," she said. "He had an accident when he was a baby. He's too young to work yet."

The guard stared at her for a moment. "Go on," he grunted. His voice had an odd note, as if his larynx was constricted.

"I didn't have an accident," said Siggy when they were inside.

"Well, you look odd to us, especially with your back," said Mia. "Sorry—you don't want to mess with them."

They walked further into the pyramid. The whole ground floor was honeycombed with hundreds of rooms. Everything was golden and shining, even the floors were made of golden flagstones.

Alf ran his hands over the walls. They were wavy and uneven, but highly polished. "This is real gold, isn't it?" he said.

Mia nodded.

All through the building thousands of people were scraping the walls with small, flat pieces of metal. Each room and hallway had dozens of people side by side. Alf watched one man working for a while. He scraped and scraped and scraped, then wiped the scraper blade on the edge of a small metal box. Alf looked into the box and saw the merest glimmer of gold at the bottom.

"How long have you been scraping?" he asked.

The man gave him a look. "That's a stupid question," he said. "You know as well as I do: a fortnight, at least."

Mia tugged Alf and led him away.

"Don't speak to people," she whispered. "And if they talk to you, act dumb, really dumb—but not so dumb that you appear beyond working."

In the center of the pyramid rose a massive stairway. It spiraled upwards around a square stairwell. All floors were accessed from here. Alf and Siggy stood in the center of the stairwell and looked up. The stairwell tapered as it rose, giving the impression of going towards infinity. At the top was a sun emblem on the ceiling.

They climbed the stairs. The next level was like the first: honeycombed with rooms and hundreds of people patiently scraping. The sound was a constant hiss. They climbed further, each floor smaller than the last, with guards posted at the stairs. They went to one of the openings in the side of the pyramid. It slanted and the lower edge was too high to look out of. These were the only light sources for the building. The light streamed into the corridor and gleamed off the polished gold. There was no furniture, no rugs, no storage rooms, nothing but solid gold.

Alf noticed people carrying their boxes carefully in their hands and climbing up floor after floor without stopping.

"Where are they taking the gold?" he asked.

"Upstairs," said Mia.

"There's a lot of gold here," said Siggy. "Tons and tons."

"Yes," said Mia. "All the gold in the world is here. All of it. They had to dig deep to get it—down to the center of the world. That's what disturbed the night beasts. That's what let them out. That's why we Instars have to be protected by the Golden Ones."

"But why are the people scraping the walls just to bring it upstairs," said Siggy. "I don't get it."

"To eat. To live. We all have to do it—except for the Golden Ones. We offer it before the upper sanctum."

"So the gold goes up, and then what?" asked Siggy.

Mia shrugged. "Then they have more of it, I suppose. The Golden Ones have a great king. The light in the gold is for him."

"What's he like?" asked Alf.

"I don't know," said Mia. "We never see the king. We never see any of the Golden Ones. Only the elevated do. Once they pass the threshold they are never seen again."

"Why not?" asked Alf.

Mia looked down and walked away.

Siggy ran after her and caught her hand. "It won't work," he said.

Mia looked at him. She didn't understand.

"What won't?"

"The pyramid," said Siggy. "The walls below are getting thinner and thinner. Up above there's more and more gold. It will collapse in the future and crush thousands."

Mia smiled and shook her head. "No," she said. "The Golden Ones are special. They are smarter than us. The pyramid will last forever. The more we serve, the more everybody will have what they need. Look around—see, everyone has work. The Golden Ones created the guards to protect all this greatness."

Alf wanted to say something, so did Siggy, but Mia walked off. She took a small box from her pocket and opened it. The lid held the scraper. She slipped it out and started scraping a wall. She was quiet and intent. Alf and Siggy watched her for a while.

"How long are you going to be?" Alf asked.

"The rest of the day," said Mia. "Don't go any further upstairs. Go back to the tilting—I've told Mama to let you in. Stay on the paths. Just don't get there past sunset. If you do, no one can let you in. No one."

Alf and Siggy ignored Mia's warning and wandered further upwards. Higher and higher they climbed until the stairway ended at the threshold to the inner sanctum of the Golden Ones. Until now the walls had been flat and bare. On this floor they are inscribed with the sun motif. Before the threshold's double doors three guards stood with folded arms. They looked exactly like the others but their uniform had golden stars on the arms. The threshold doors were of solid gold too. They were ornately cast, with scenes and symbols in the panels. To either side were long, golden tables manned by guards. A line of people wound down the stairs and into the hallway of the next level. When they reached the table they handed their box to a guard who weighed it and gave them a piece of paper and a new box. Then they left, walking slowly down the stairs.

Alf and Siggy felt the guards watching them. No doubt they were wondering why they were here and yet had nothing to hand in.

"Hey, you," called a guard, walking towards them. "You with the pointy-eared kid. Come here."

Alf froze. He didn't know what to do. Siggy, however, instantly waltzed up to the guard, fell on his knees and licked his boots. The guard was too stunned to do anything except stare. Alf grabbed Siggy and hauled him away.

"Sorry," he called over his shoulder. "He had an accident. He's very helpful ... just a little stupid sometimes ... you know ..." and he fled down the stairs with Siggy in tow.

They expected the guard to chase them or raise the alarm, but nothing happened. They looked for Mia but couldn't find her. They'd forgotten which floor she was on. They found their way outside, but didn't recognize where they were and had to circle the building. The white stone landing extended around the whole base, and each of the four sides had an identical grand avenue. Finally they recognized the way they'd come in and wandered down the hill, looking at the crops. They spied what looked like an orchard with fruit hanging from the branches.

"Let's go there," said Siggy, and headed over without waiting for Alf.

He hadn't gone far when a mottled, green and brown animal darted out from underneath a bush and stood in front of him. It was as large as a dog, with a wide head and mouth.

Siggy stopped, unsure what to do.

"Nice animal," he said, hopefully.

The animal changed color to dirty red. It hissed and showed fangs. Siggy backed away, the animal following him until he reached the main path. As soon as he was on the path the animal changed color and trotted back to its bush. It was almost impossible to see when it lay underneath.

"I guess the food is guarded," said Alf.

"I guess so too," said Siggy, holding his tummy. "But if I don't eat soon I'll die. And I do mean die!"

16 – Night Forest

Alf and Siggy wandered through the forest. They kept to the paths. Despite what they'd heard in the night they didn't really understand Mia's concern about walking in the forest. It was so peaceful and quiet—and beautiful where the trees were in flower. They were fragrant. But it was easier to walk on the paths so that's where they stayed. Overhead, the sun had grown to its maximum when they got back to the tilting. It was a lovely golden yellow hue.

Siggy knocked on the door. The peephole slid back and an eye looked out.

"It's us, Mama," said Alf.

The eye stared.

"What do you want?" asked a man's voice.

"We're friends with Mia," said Alf. "She said Mama would let us in."

"There's no Mama and no Mia here," said the gatekeeper, and the peephole slid shut.

Alf and Siggy stepped back and looked at the tilting. It seemed similar, but they couldn't be sure. They walked about and examined it carefully. It wasn't the same one. They'd taken a wrong turn in the forest. It all looked the same to them. Alf went back to the door and knocked. The peephole opened and the eye stared at them for a second. Then it closed and wouldn't open no matter what Alf said.

Alf and Siggy tried to retrace their steps, but the forest paths wandered up and down and around the rolling landscape. If one part seemed familiar, they'd turn a corner and it was clear they'd never been there before. Surprisingly, the tiltings, for all their great height, were hard to see through the trees. Only when they were close to one did it peek through the canopy. They tried another tilting, then another, but the keepers didn't know Mia and wouldn't let them in.

"Let's go back to Golden Hill," said Siggy. "We'll look for Mia there," but the pyramid was impossible to see from the forest. So they climbed a hill, the tallest they could find, but only caught a glimmer of gold beyond the leaves.

"Wait here," said Alf, and climbed a tree. He climbed until he could look out over the landscape. The tall tiltings rose upwards to the sky, and there in the distance gleamed the pyramid. It reflected the reddening sun, one facet catching the light and shining brightly.

"I see it," shouted Alf down to Siggy. "We've gone too far."

Alf looked some more, but from here he couldn't tell which was the right tilting. Off to one side, however, was a hill with a large tree dominating the top.

"I think I saw the tree we came out of," said Alf when he got down. "Let's try there. We'll have to be quick. The sun is reddening. I don't think we have much time."

Alf and Siggy jogged through the forest. Siggy had difficulty keeping up. He was weak and his legs short.

"Hurry," said Alf. "We can't be out in the dark."

"I'm trying," said Siggy. "Having a body is a real drag."

The paths they were on kept turning away from where they wanted to go. Now and then they came across people hurrying along. They tried to stop them to ask the way to the tree, but they shook their heads and kept going.

"Get home, get home," some of them urged. "Get to your tilting!" But Alf and Siggy didn't know the name of Mia's tilting and none knew Mia.

They found the hill and left the path and went directly towards the tree. Roots caught their feet and branches scratched their faces as they wound in and out of the undergrowth. Twilight was settling in as they neared the crest. Suddenly the tree loomed above them, it's strangely naked, root-like branches silhouetted against the shrinking sun. They ran around the trunk. There was no opening. It wasn't the right one.

Alf eyes glowed in the red light. He was afraid. Siggy was afraid too.

"We have to climb up," said Siggy. "We can't stay down here."

They searched for a tree that Siggy could climb, but their best bet was the big tree. It had vines growing up the trunk as thick as a man's wrist. Alf lifted Siggy as high as he could and followed. They wedged their feet into cracks and crevices and pulled themselves up.

"This is ridiculous," said Siggy, panting heavily. "It's so much easier to have wings and go wherever you send your thoughts."

"Stop complaining and keep climbing," said Alf. "You're the one who misused your silly magic."

High above the ground the branches spread out from the trunk. Here there was room to rest securely.

The leaves above them rustled and shook. They looked up and saw two oaplahs half-floating, half-crawling in the canopy. They worked their way to the topmost branches and hung on with one tentacle. Already their eyelids were drooping as if falling asleep. A smaller animal with large grey eyes and a tail came down a branch and stared at them for a while. Then it leaped across to another tree and left. 'Kee-ree! Kee-ree!' cried the birds, darting through the trees in a frenzy of activity.

Night came on rapidly and utter darkness fell. The air cooled and dampness rose from the ground. All sounds stopped. Alf and Siggy waited. It didn't take long. The forest floor rustled and there were footsteps. Something crawled by, as if on many legs. The forest felt alive, the air tense. Someone walked around the trunk. Others came. Different ones. They had trouble breathing. They labored. Some wheezed. Others snorted. Then came a cry—like a pig being stuck in the throat with a butcher's knife. It went on and on in terror. It was off to one side. Footsteps hurried in that direction and the screams became louder. Then they ceased.

Alf and Siggy hardly dared to breathe. Alf found himself wishing for the moon. There was no moon, nor stars.

The night wore on. The creatures below came and went. More screams. Some near, some far. One climbed a tree beside them. It was big. When it reached the canopy it systematically shook the branches. The air shifted and a foul smell wafted over. It was penetrating. An animal in the tree tops tried to make an escape. They heard it cry out and scramble along a branch. It must have leaped or lost its grip for it suddenly fell. There was a dull thud. The hunter scurried down from the tree with startling speed.

There was a brief cry; then gnashing and grinding. Alf and Siggy waited for the hunter to leave, but he never did, not that they could hear.

Hours passed, their tension draining them. Alf's head nodded now and then. He realized that he might fall asleep through sheer exhaustion. He was afraid to sleep, even for an instant. What if he made a noise, or fell? What then?

Later in the night Alf became aware of something moving down a branch towards them. He sensed rather than saw it. It wasn't large. He reached out and took Siggy's hand. Siggy squeezed twice. He sensed it too. About ten feet away it stopped. They knew it was there, but couldn't see or hear it. They waited, stiff and tense, wondering what it was and whether they should leap or fight if attacked. At last the sky lightened by a fraction. Alf realized he could see the tracery of the branches. He stared at the spot where the animal lurked. Only a shape, a lump, could be seen.

Footsteps below scurried and hastened. The forest litter was stirred and cast about. Then silence. Silence fell as the deeply red sun appeared in a dark, dark blue sky

Siggy tugged at Alf's shirt. He did it so softly that Alf hardly noticed. They could see the animal on the branch now. It had begun to move towards them. It emitted a faint, throbbing sound; warm, like a purr. Suddenly Alf knew what it was. It was a cat-bird. He relaxed and Siggy shot him a look.

"Come here, Kitty-o," Alf called, his voice barely audible. He was afraid to speak loudly.

The cat-bird stretched and yawned. It opened its wings and reached forward with its forelegs and scratched the tree. Then it came towards Alf, purring loudly.

"It is Kitty-o," said Alf, reaching out to stroke her.

"How can you be sure?" said Siggy.

"Well, if it's not, then it has the same name and it has a star on its head," said Alf, scratching her behind the ears. He was amazed at the transformation Kitty-o had undergone. He didn't understand how it was possible. Her body was lighter and her wings were soft and covered with downy fur.

The cat-bird curled up in Alf's lap and licked her coat. Then she dozed. Alf laid his head against a branch. He was spent. In an instant he was asleep.

17 – Back

"Alf! Siggy!" a voice called.

Alf woke with a start. Kitty-o stirred in his lap. The sun had grown to orange. Siggy was sound asleep, his arms around a branch. A twig snapped below them. Kitty-o sat up, suddenly alert. She leaped onto a branch and looked towards the ground.

"Kew! Kew!" she cried.

"Asa," called Mia from below, surprised. "What are you doing here? Where were you last night?"

"Kew!" said Asa.

Alf looked down.

"There you are," said Mia, relieved. "I've been tracking you for ages. Is Siggy still alive too?"

Alf nodded. "Yes, we're both here." He shook Siggy's shoulder, then shook him again. He had a hard time waking up. He'd grown an inch or two. He was thin and pale.

"I have to eat," said Siggy. "I must drink."

"We'll climb down," said Alf—but it wasn't easy. Siggy was weak and Mia had to climb up to help get him out of the tree.

Once they were on the ground Mia didn't hang around. "Let's go," she said, walking off.

"Where are you going?" said Alf.

"To the path. I'm bringing you back to my tilting."

Alf shook his head. "No, Siggy needs to eat. We have to go back to the tree we came from."

Mia hesitated.

"We must," said Alf, "unless you can feed him lots—and I mean lots."

"I can't do that," said Mia. "I'll have to take you to the tree."

Alf carried Siggy on his back as Mia meandered through the forest. She stopped now and then, and turned left and right randomly.

"What are you doing?" said Alf. "Just go, he's getting heavy."

"No," said Mia. "I told you, when you're off the path you have to be careful."

"Of what?"

Mia's mouth dropped. "Weren't you here last night?"

Alf blushed. He felt stupid.

"Where do you think they come from?" she said, gesturing to the ground. "I told you they came from underneath." She resumed her cautious weaving through the trees. "There are lots around here." She stopped and pointed to a clearing. "There, for instance."

Alf put Siggy down. Neither of them saw anything.

"I don't see ... " Alf began.

"Look!" said Mia.

Alf looked, but wasn't sure what to look for.

"The rise," said Mia, gesturing.

Alf saw that one part of the clearing was slightly domed; a rough circle about ten feet across. The forest litter was stirred up; it looked fresher there.

"Where it's domed?" asked Alf.

"Yes," said Mia. "That's one place. They're under there."

"So that's why the leaf litter is fresh."

Mia nodded. "That helps, but only for a while. By mid morning you won't be able to tell the difference."

"So, look for the domes," said Siggy.

"Yes," said Mia. "But by this afternoon even the domes are gone."

"Then what?" asked Siggy.

"Then you have to be lucky," said Mia. "Stay on the path, we keep them cleared of leaves. But even there you have to be sharp."

They wandered on, Mia taking her time and only going forwards when she was sure. At last they came to a path and their pace quickened. Alf couldn't keep up with Siggy on his back.

"I'm thirsty," moaned Siggy. "I have to drink."

Alf was thirsty too. "We'll get back soon," he reassured Siggy, setting him down for a moment.

Mia put Siggy onto her back and they went faster.

"What's the rush?" asked Alf. He had to push himself to keep up.

"I need to eat too," said Mia. "Look at the sun. If I don't work, I don't eat. Simple. You two ate all my food. Half the day will be gone before I get to the pyramid."

Finally they walked up a steep hill. Near the top Alf made out the large tree, but from the path it looked no different to the one they'd spent the night in. Mia slowed down and left the path. She made her way to the tree, circled it, and checked inside the trunk. This was the right one. Then she put Siggy down.

"Are you sure you came from here?" she asked.

"Come look," said Alf, leading the way inside the trunk.

To one side was the hole in the ground. It was partly filled with leaves. Mia's eyes widened. She looked wildly into the hole and then at Alf and Siggy.

"You came from underneath?" she said, suddenly distrustful.

"We came out that hole," said Alf, "but I know we didn't come from what you call underneath. Whatever beasts were in the jungle last night don't live in my world."

Mia relaxed.

"We told you, there's a passage," said Alf. "It's silvery. We come from another world. It's different."

Alf stopped. Then he heard himself pleading: "Come with us, Mia."

Mia's look of fear was answer enough.

Siggy fainted without warning. He keeled over and hit the ground with a thud. He was so pale. Alf and Mia bent over him, patting his face and calling his name. Kitty-o walked in from outside. She'd stayed in the tree when Alf and Siggy left with Mia. She must have followed. She licked Siggy's face.

"Kew, kew," she cried plaintively.

Siggy's eyelids fluttered and he woke up. "I saw ice cream," he said. "Lots of ice cream. I was licking it."

"What's ice cream?" asked Mia. "Is it medicine?"

"It's made from creamy milk," said Alf.

"And sugar," said Siggy, "lots of sugar."

"You freeze it, and stir it," said Alf, "and then … "

"What's milk?" asked Mia.

"Never mind. We have to go. We can't stay."

Worry and fear crossed Mia's face again. She stood back.

Alf climbed into the hole and helped Siggy down. He looked up to see Mia by the doorway in the tree trunk. She was trembling. She turned and fled. Alf heard her footsteps fleeing through the forest. She was running heedless of danger.

"Come on," said Alf, bending over and entering the passage.

They walked down the short slope and turned the corner towards the door. It had a sign: a red hand, palm facing forwards. Alf stopped and Siggy bumped into him. They were surprised. They'd both missed seeing the sign on this side.

"Let's go," said Siggy. He was so weak that nothing but food and drink mattered to him.

Alf reached out and gripped the door handle. He had to pull hard to swing the door open.

18 – Chosen One

"Where the stinking fish have you two been?" asked Cam when they came out of the Hall. "We've been looking everywhere."

"Siggy's hungry," said Alf. "And thirsty."

"Serves him right," said Cam, looking Alf up and down. "And you too if you're hungry."

Cam turned and marched off through the carnival. It was late morning and the crowds were thickening. He stopped and looked back. "Come on! Come on!" he shouted.

Alf took Siggy's hand and led him after Cam. They came to Ester's Eatery. Ester was cleaning up after making breakfast for the vendors. She rushed over when she saw Siggy.

"What have you done to him?" she cried, giving Cam a dirty look.

"Me?" said Cam, already leaving. "They vanished into thin air and then waltzed out of the Hall. I had nothing to do with it."

Ester paid him no attention but gave Siggy a glass of water and a banana. Then she began to fry eggs and sausages. Alf helped himself to whatever food was lying around and sat down. Siggy scarfed the food on his plate and asked for more. His pallor improved immediately.

"I needed this sooooooooooo bad," he said.

"Me too," said Alf.

They sat eating in silence for a long time, too tired to speak.

"So where have you two been?" asked Ester, sitting down with them. "Looks like you've been climbing trees," and she picked a leaf off Alf's back. She examined it carefully.

Alf glanced at Siggy. "It's hard to describe," he said.

"Let me guess," said Ester, still eyeing the leaf, "perhaps a place with a golden pyramid?"

Alf and Siggy stared at her.

"How did you know?" asked Siggy.

"You get an eye for these things after a while," said Ester. "Appearing, disappearing, but mostly the kind of leaves people carry on their backs."

"There were monsters," said Siggy. "We spent the night in the forest."

"Then you're lucky to be here," said Ester. She watched Siggy eating. "Slow down," she chided. "You'll catch a stomachache."

"How do you know about that place?" asked Alf. "We never did find out what it's called."

"Instar—same as the people," said Ester, "though some call it by other names. When I was a teenager I found a place in the forest by accident—a hollow tree on a hill. I crawled inside and fell into a passage. I never went back."

"Why not?" asked Siggy.

"I was chosen, but I escaped the guards and ran away. I don't know what happened to the rest of my family, but I couldn't return." Ester's gaze was far away, remembering a distant past. "I was lucky, I suppose. At least I don't have to listen to the beasts at night. And I like helping people. I help and I live. It's enough for me."

Siggy's head was sinking towards his plate. His eyes were closed and his fork hung in the air half way to his mouth.

Ester grinned. "Time for a snooze," she said, taking the fork. "I'll give you a haircut later. You look like a floor mop."

The Darkling Beasts

Alf and Siggy made their way back to Cam and his mum. They were busy with customers. Alf took Siggy to the cab of the Hall truck. Somehow they found room for two on the bench seat and fell asleep.

19 – Two Meals

Siggy was now four feet tall and a whole week old.

"When are you going to stop growing," said Cam. It was supper and Siggy was eating up a storm again.

"Tomorrow morning," said Siggy. "One more inch and I'm done."

"Right!" scoffed Cam. "And how do you know that?"

"I have psychosomatic control mechanisms," said Siggy, looking Cam in the eye.

Cam hesitated. He wasn't sure what the words meant.

"It means because I've decided to," said Siggy. "Forty-nine inches is a good size. Big enough for me—for now at least."

"Why forty-nine?" asked Cam.

"'Coz it's seven times seven," said Siggy.

"Fine," said Cam, annoyed. "Stop when you want."

A moment's silence followed. Alf looked out the restaurant window. It was raining and many stalls had closed early. Cam's mum was looking after the Hall of Mirrors. It was popular in wet weather. People went in to get out of the rain and have a bit of fun. Alf wondered how carnival people could make a reliable living without reliable weather. He looked across at Cam and realized for the first time that the cheap clothes he wore might not just be bad taste.

"More desert," said Siggy. He'd already had two ice creams.

"No," said Alf. "That's enough."

Siggy gave Alf a look, but kept quiet.

They sat as Cam drank his tea. "Okay," he said at last, getting up. "Let's see if we can earn a clinker or two on this lovely evening."

*　*　*

"What are you doing?" asked Siggy.

"Collecting," said Alf. It was night; the rain had stopped, and the carnival was in full swing. He'd found an old canvas shopping bag and was stuffing it with food. He begged an apple here, an orange there, whatever the carnival folk would give him. Circles, the Ferris wheel owner, gave him a whole submarine.

"That sub's for me, I bet," said Siggy, putting his hand into the bag.

Alf slapped it away.

"Who's it for then?" said Siggy.

"Mia."

"You're going back!" exclaimed Siggy. "That's nuts."

"I'm going," said Alf, his jaw set. "I'd hoped you'd come ... well, presumed, actually."

"There's no food there," said Siggy, "not to mention it's dangerous. When do we go?"

"Tonight."

"Tonight! We've only had two meals and a lousy nap in the truck cab."

"Why wait?" said Alf, walking to the next vendor. "Besides, tomorrow the carnival ups pegs and we might not get such an easy chance back at Cam's mum's place."

20 – Instar

"I've lost my key," said Cam's mum, rooting in her purse. Her hair was in plastic curlers and she was wearing a jaded pink bathrobe which barely contained her rotund self.

Siggy didn't flinch and kept his face stuck in his book. He'd begged it at a secondhand book shop. It was stained and the back cover missing so they'd given it to him for free. It was called, *'Birds: Statistical Probability of Randomly Evolving towards Feathered Flight'*, by A. D. Saurus, PhD., PhD.

"Who's seen my Hall key?" said Cam's mum again.

Alf didn't flinch either. He rolled over on the bed and pretended to read over Siggy's shoulder. He didn't understand a word. Finally Cam's mum gave up looking and sat on her bed. She read a magazine called 'Beauty'. It had a plastic woman on the cover.

The Darkling Beasts

"Hey, Alf," called Cam, throwing a wad of paper at him from the armchair. "What's that bag of food for?"

"Siggy," said Alf, without looking up. "In case he gets hungry in the night."

"Good one," said Cam, and went back to cleaning his nails with his army knife.

Finally everyone settled. Alf was tired; he was worried he'd fall asleep—which he did in short order. Siggy shook him awake. The luminous clock said two thirty-three. Cam and his mum were snoring in unison.

"It's time," Siggy whispered.

Alf sat up, disoriented. It took a moment to remember where he was. He slipped on his shoes and jacket and grabbed the bag. "Come on," he said, and out the door they went.

Siggy ate an apple as they walked through the streets. Everything was damp from a passing shower. They came to the Hall of Mirrors and opened the door. They locked it behind them and walked down the passages. This time Siggy had brought a key ring flashlight he'd snitched. It had a tiny but powerful bulb. They turned right, then right, then right again. There was the door. The sign said, 'DON'T'.

Alf hesitated. So did Siggy.

"We have to go," said Alf, and he touched the handle. The door swung open. This time they checked the sign on the other side. It was still there, but scratched, as if by claws. They closed the door. It resisted them. They came to the end of the silver tunnel and stopped. There was noise; beasts were roaming; they could hear them clearly. They went back to the door but it wouldn't open.

"Now what?" said Siggy in a told-you-so voice. He was frightened and wished he hadn't come.

"We wait," said Alf as casually as possible and sat down on the floor.

From the door the night sounds were faint and far away, as if the passage was longer than it seemed. Still, what the sounds spoke was clear enough. They stayed where they were and avoided looking at the claw marks on the door behind them. They must have slept because the next thing they remembered was Kitty-o purring and rubbing against their legs. She still had her wings.

Outside the tree trunk the sun was small but waxing. They made their way downhill followed by Kitty-o. They had been so innocent the last time they'd come, casually sauntering through the forest and taking in the sights. This time they were cautious. They peered ahead intently, seeking out the telling signs. They were about to cross a clearing when Kitty-o mewed and ran ahead. She turned and opened her wings, blocking their way. Alf got on his hunkers and looked more closely. There it was, the slight bulge. He hadn't seen a thing standing up—and besides, the ground was uneven. How were you supposed to tell the difference?

Siggy brought up the rear. He'd snitched Cam's army knife and was cutting a blaze on every tree they passed. When they needed to come back they'd retrace their steps, if they survived.

Kitty-o led the way from then on. She wove an erratic line through trees until they reached a path. Then she sprinted downhill and took to the air.

"Thanks," called Alf, grateful for being brought to safety.

"Thanks," called Siggy, annoyed that she hadn't stayed.

They wandered down the hill. Now and then they met people or saw them through the trees. They were all going towards Golden Hill. They reached Mia's tilting, sure this time that it was the right one. They knocked and an eye looked out the spy-hole. Immediately the gate opened. It was Mama.

"You've come back to Nova tilting," she said in surprise. "Mia said you'd gone, but wouldn't tell me where. She was upset."

"We had to go away," said Alf. "We didn't have a choice."

Mama nodded.

"What's in your bag?" she asked.

Alf showed her.

"Looks like food—but none I've ever seen."

Alf gave her an apple. She held it in her hands and turned it over.

"Is it safe," she asked.

Siggy nodded. "If you don't want it, I'll eat it," he said.

Mama grinned and took a bite. Her eyes lit up.

"It's sweet," she said. "And crunchy."

Alf and Siggy smiled as she slowly ate the apple. She ate it as if it was a never-granted luxury.

The Darkling Beasts

"Where's Mia," asked Alf at last.

"Scraping," said Mama. "Perhaps you should wait."

So they did.

21 – Orange and Meat

Late in the afternoon they heard Mia's footsteps climbing the stairs. Siggy ran to the door and opened it.

"Surprise!" he called out childishly.

Mia grinned. "No surprise," she said. "Mama told me already. But I'm glad you're still alive."

"We brought you food," said Alf, holding out the bag.

"But some's for me, too," said Siggy.

Alf clouted him across the back of the head.

Mia took the food out of the bag and laid it on the table.

"Can you really eat this?" she asked, holding out an orange. "It's so bright. It looks like the sun at halfshine."

"Try it," said Alf.

Before they could stop her she'd bitten into the skin.

"Wait," cried Alf and Siggy in unison.

Mia stopped in mid bite. "Why?" she asked. "It's delicious."

"You're supposed to peel it," said Siggy.

Alf took it from her and peeled the skin off. He gave her a segment. Her eyes lit up.

"It's sweet and zingy at the same time," she said, eating slowly and savoring it. "Our food is plain."

Siggy wanted a piece too, so Alf gave him one.

"Can we save some for later?" asked Mia. "I don't want to eat it all now."

"Yes," said Alf, "but not for long. It might go bad."

Mia took some orange skin and nibbled on it. She liked it too.

"We don't eat it," said Alf. "It stings," but Mia just shrugged.

"What food goes bad first?" she asked.

Siggy pointed to the submarine. "It used to be bigger," he said with a semblance of an apology, "but I had to have lunch."

"Let's all eat," said Mia.

So they sat on a blanket on the floor and divided the sandwich.

"What's this red stuff?" asked Mia, after a moment. "It tastes odd."

"Ham," said Alf.

"From pig," said Siggy when she looked puzzled.

She still looked puzzled.

"It's an animal from our world," said Alf.

Mia stopped chewing.

"A beast?" she asked.

Alf didn't know what to say.

"A good one," said Siggy.

"You eat good beasts?" asked Mia. She didn't like what she was hearing.

"Yes," said Alf at last. "Most people do."

"I don't eat good animals," said Mia with finality, putting the sandwich away from her. "And I don't eat the bad ones either. They smell of death."

She got up, walked to a window and gazed out. After a moment Siggy ate her sandwich.

Alf gave him a look. "I thought you'd stopped growing," he said.

"I'm still a kid," said Siggy. "Kids are supposed to be hungry."

Alf rolled his eyes.

"What kind of place do you come from?" asked Mia at last, coming back to the picnic.

"It's different," said Alf. "Almost everything is different, but especially the sun."

"How can you eat good animals?" she asked. She seemed distant and distracted.

Just then a flurry of wings filled the window.

"Kew! Kew!" mewed a cat-bird, leaping into the room. It had a star on its forehead.

"Kitty-o!" cried Alf and Siggy.

"Asa!" cried Mia at the same time.

"So you do know her," said Mia. "I was surprised that she was with you in the tree. I thought she was there by chance. She's very friendly."

"We know her," said Alf. "She guided us safely through the forest this morning."

The Darkling Beasts

"She comes to our world too," said Siggy, "but there she doesn't have wings."

"She goes to your world?" said Mia. "And has no wings? That's impossible."

"Kew! Kew!" called Kitty-o plaintively, trying to get their full attention.

Alf shrugged. "She comes to us, and she doesn't have wings. None of our cats do. Is she yours?"

"We don't own animals," said Mia. "If they like us we appreciate it. If not, then there's nothing to be done about it."

The light was fading fast from the room. Alf wanted to see the sun vanish for the night and climbed up the ladder. He stood on the roof and looked around. A gentle breeze swayed the building back and forth. Alf didn't dare stand close to the edge—the parapet was only knee high. In the distance the golden pyramid gleamed. The air was crystal clear this evening and he could see further than before. Off to one side was a line of sandy color with an edge of white. It looked like a beach. Beyond it a grayish-blue melted into a purer blue.

Alf lay down and gazed upwards as the sun shrank to a point directly above his head. He felt light and weightless. At the last moment the sun's light became hazy and dissolved into the air. Finally it winked out and the darkness was total. It caught him by surprise and he had to fumble for the ladder. He climbed down and closed the hatch. Before he'd reached the last step the night beasts were howling and hunting below.

22 – *To the Sea*

"I thought I saw the sea last night," said Alf. "Let's go."

It was morning and the sunlight was strengthening.

"It is the sea," said Mia. "It's all around. I'd go, but I have to work."

"Everyday?" asked Siggy.

"Yes."

"We have food," said Alf. "No one is forcing you. We can bring it."

"True," said Mia. "The Golden Ones have given us freedom. Instar is the land of freedom."

So they went.

In the forest the birds were singing in the treetops: yellow ones, red ones, white ones with long orange beaks. Some were as big as crows, but most were smaller. Mia stopped now and then to listen. She liked them.

"There's a teee-la bird," she said, pointing to a speckled pink and light green bird with a long tail and pointed beak. It hopped from branch to branch pecking at insects. "Their young will be fledged soon."

After a couple of miles they rounded a corner and the path halted abruptly. They had to bypass a tilting. It had fallen over and lay crumpled and broken. A makeshift trail passed between two segments. They could see through some of the windows into the rooms, now filled with vines and undergrowth.

"When did this fall?" asked Alf.

"Two summers ago," said Mia. "My friend, Sattia, was inside. A storm blew it over. The summer storms can be vicious."

Siggy scampered into one of the rooms and looked around. There were bones.

"Don't," said Mia. "We leave the dead alone. It's better that way."

Further on the trees changed. They became dark and heavy leaved. Some had spiky bark. They were in a narrow valley. The ground was tossed and heaved. Huge holes and pits, now overgrown, could be seen on either side. The air was close and dense and a foul smell lingered which was hard to ignore. There were no tiltings to be seen.

Mia hurried ahead. "We can't stay here for long," she said, and Alf and Siggy didn't argue.

They climbed out of the valley and into the next. The dark trees fell away. The wind was stronger and the vegetation spaced further apart. The hillside below them was covered with large boulders. They were a deep, rich red. The path wound down through the boulders, then up again. The wind picked up even more as they neared the crest of the next ridge. They could smell the sea. Mia stopped and gazed ahead.

"The ocean," she said, with a grand sweep of her arm.

Alf and Siggy stood speechless; before them lay the ocean, curving gently upwards into the sky. The wind was brisk; it whitened the waves with sea horses until the eye gave out and, horizonless, the sky began.

"What's happening?" asked Alf.

The Darkling Beasts

"I don't know," said Siggy. "It's the opposite, I think."

"The opposite of what?" asked Mia, not understanding their confusion.

"To our world," said Alf. "Our sea is flat—or at least it looks flat. Our world is round—but it's big and so the sea looks flat."

"Instar is round too," said Mia.

"Yes, but you live on the inside; we live on the outside."

Mia stared at him.

"How big is your world?" asked Siggy.

"To us it's big," said Mia. "This land is the only one in the great ocean."

"What happens if you sail away?" asked Alf.

"They say you come back on the other side. At least that's what the stories tell. Men wanted to see if there was another land. Some came back in weeks, depending on the wind. Most didn't come back at all. Now we are not allowed to build boats. The Golden Ones say it's for our safety."

Alf sat on the ground and held his head. He was trying to work it out. "Your sun is at the center of your world," he said, drawing a circle in the dirt and putting a point in the center.

"Of course," said Mia.

"It never rises on one side and sets on the other."

"That's impossible," said Mia. "The sun waxes and wanes daily, and in summer it is bigger and hotter; in winter it is smaller and cooler. Don't you have summer and winter too?"

"Yes," said Alf, "but … "

"There you go," said Mia, taking off down the hill like a deer.

23 – *Swimming*

Alf and Siggy stood on the beach and looked out at the sea. It was so similar, and yet so different. Then they ran down the strand, playing in the surf and building sandcastles.

"Do you have tides?" Siggy suddenly asked, but Mia didn't know the word.

"When the sea rises and falls," said Siggy. "Those are tides."

"Only with the storms," said Mia.

"How about a moon?" asked Alf, and Mia shook her head.

They walked towards a rocky headland. When they reached it there were pools aplenty, but only seaweed grew in them.

"Where's all the life?" asked Alf, disappointed.

"My mother told me there used to be lots of life on Instar," said Mia.

"What happened?" asked Siggy.

"It was used up. Now our food is supplied by the Beautiful Golden Ones."

"Speaking of food," said Siggy, opening the shopping bag and peering in.

They had lunch in the shelter of a cove backed by a short, steep cliff. Here a rugged coast began, with small rocky islands not far offshore. Siggy, for once, didn't eat so ravenously.

"So what's up with you, Pigster?" asked Alf.

"I told you," said Siggy. "Today I stop growing. I'm big enough, for now."

Alf examined Siggy carefully. He looked like a child ... sort of. He was slim and wiry, with slanted, cheeky eyes and pointy ears.

"Why the pointy ears?" asked Alf, reaching out and giving one a tug.

"'Coz we're not you," said Siggy, whacking his hand away. "Who'd want round, dumbo ears anyway?"

Alf snorted; he'd never looked at it that way.

*　*　*

Alf lay on the beach gazing up at the sky. It drew him upwards and he had to close his eyes now and then to recenter himself. He was still trying to get used to the sun always being in one place. He couldn't understand how it appeared and disappeared.

"Siggy," said Alf, "how does this sun appear and disappear and always be in one place. I can't work it out."

"I think their sun's a luminous, four-dimensional sphere which passes through an internalized three dimensional space," said Siggy. "That's how it appears and disappears."

The Darkling Beasts

"And what does Professor Singular mean by that?" asked Alf, but Siggy had gotten up and was running down the beach shouting, "Waaaaaaves! Waaaaaaves! Waaaaaaves!" His arms were flung out as if he was trying to embrace the whole world.

Alf chuckled and lay down on the sand again. His shoes were off and he dug into the warm sand with his toes. Mia was lying next to him and making sand angels. Alf closed his eyes and listened. The waves beat on the shore, the beach shaking slightly with each boom. The wind whipped and played with his hair and for a while he relaxed completely.

Suddenly Mia sat up. "Where's Siggy?" she asked.

Alf opened his eyes and turned his head. No Siggy. He sat up and looked around. Still no Siggy.

"Siggy! Siggy" he called. "Siggy!"

No reply.

"There he is," said Mia. "Oh, no—Siggy!"

Siggy was in the water hanging onto a log. Alf jumped up and ran down the beach. "Siggy! Siggy!" he called.

Siggy waved.

"What are you doing?" shouted Alf.

"Swimming," said Siggy.

"I didn't know you could swim," said Alf.

"I can't. I was trying to learn."

"Get back here," shouted Alf. "You're too far out."

"Can't," he called. "There's a current."

Siggy paddled with his legs, but the log made no headway and floated further out. Alf ran into the waves and swam towards the log. The breakers knocked him back a few times before he was clear of them. He glanced back to shore. He was much further out than he should be, the current must be strong. The water was colder offshore, and the wind made him colder still. He began to shiver when he reached the log.

"Kick," he said, and they both kicked, trying to move the log towards land. Soon they had to give up. They were only wasting their energy. Alf looked around. The current was drawing them towards a rocky islet.

"Let's go there if we can," said Alf, and they swung the log around and moved with the current. Finally they were making progress. When they reached the islet they barely had the strength to fight the surging waves and haul themselves onto the rocks.

"Help me keep the log," said Alf, trying to wrestle it onto the island, "without it we'll never get off this place."

They struggled mightily, but Siggy was too weak and Alf was not strong enough by himself.

"Leave it," said Alf. "It's no use."

They sat on the rock panting and shivering and watched the log drift away. Mia stood on the shore, one hand shading her eyes. She stayed there for a long time. She shouted, but the wind blew her words away. Finally she left and Alf and Siggy had the whole place to themselves.

24 – *Stranded*

Alf and Siggy huddled in a crevice out of the wind. Their clothes had partly dried but they were still cold. The afternoon was wearing on and the light was visibly waning.

"The wind's dropping," said Siggy, "Perhaps we could swim."

Alf looked doubtful. He tossed a stick far out onto the water and watched as it drifted quickly out to sea.

"It's not the wind we have to fear," he said, coming back, "it's the current."

There was lots of driftwood and seaweed and they improvised a shelter in one of the crevices. It was reasonably cozy and out of the wind. As long as it didn't rain they'd be okay.

Dusk came. It was strange to have a 'sunset' without a setting and without long shadows. Then, in an instant, night fell; fully, as if the light of the world had been switched off. From the land, the night howling, muted and distant, crossed the water to them. Alf and Siggy shivered when they heard it.

"I don't want to be outside ever again in this place at night," said Siggy.

"Then don't do stupid things," said Alf. He was annoyed.

"Stupid as in coming back to this weird world in the first place?" asked Siggy.

The Darkling Beasts

Alf said nothing. He tried to sleep, but it was hard. He must have dozed off because he woke with Siggy tugging at him.

"Look! Come look!" he said.

Siggy led him onto the rocks. The wind had dropped and a silvery light glimmered faintly on the waves. Alf looked up. The night was clear and filled with stars.

"Look," said Siggy in wonder.

"Stars," said Alf.

"No, look!" insisted Siggy.

Alf looked more carefully. The lights, the stars, were rising out of the ocean. Only at a glance did they look like stars. Thousands and thousands of lights were rising up through the water and floating into the air. They moved slowly, steadily, and in great numbers into the sky. It was majestic. Soon everything glowed silver, as if under a bright full moon. Alf could see the inward curve of the world, for far out to sea the lights rose upwards at a different angle. They all floated towards the great central point of Instar. A breeze picked up and the lights gathered into swirls and rivers and galaxies.

"It's the wind," said Siggy. "The wind is streaming them."

The wind blew the lights inland and out of sight into the heights. They began to change hue, not all at once but singly, then in groups. First some took on a faint blue hue, then they became blue-green, yellow, orange-red and finally violet before suddenly winking out.

After an hour no more lights came out of the sea. A while later there were no silvery ones, then no blue-green, or yellow, or orange-red ones. Last of all the sky was dotted with violet lights floating in the heights. Finally, darkness returned. Only then did Alf and Siggy notice the bestial howling in the forest begin again.

"Whatever those monsters are," said Siggy, "they don't like light."

Alf and Siggy didn't trust themselves on two legs in the dark so they crawled on their hands and knees over the rocks back into their shelter. Just as they got there a great, guttural roar sounded from the shore. It seemed to be directed towards them.

"Do you think it saw us?" asked Siggy.

"No," said Alf—but he was lying.

25 – Back to Shore

Morning found Alf and Siggy cold and tired. They had slept in snatches, but that was all. Alf was the first up. He scouted the island. There were lots of twigs and small branches but no logs. He tossed a stick into the sea. It made its way towards shore, blown by the gentle breeze.

"Siggy," he called, "the current has shifted. Let's go. Now's our chance."

Siggy crawled out of the shelter. He looked haggard. His red hair was all over the place. He wasn't a happy camper. Alf took off his shirt and stuffed it full of dry branches and tied the lot together with the arms. He wanted to do the same with Siggy's shirt but he refused to take it off. Finally Alf gave up.

"You hold onto my shirt and don't let go," said Alf. "I'll tow, you kick. Don't forget to kick."

They got into the water, loathing the cold but grateful that the wind and waves were low. Alf swam sideways, towing the bundle and Siggy along. When they reached the breakers one picked them up and tumbled them head over heels into the shallows. Alf didn't let go of Siggy. He hauled him spluttering and coughing out of the water and onto the beach. He kept on dragging him till they reached the shelter of a dry sand dune. He collapsed, his chest heaving.

They hadn't been there long when Mia appeared. "So there you are," she said, looking down on them. "Fish! You think you're fish!" and she gave Alf a kick.

Siggy sprung to life and got behind Alf. With Mia was a crowd of people. They stared silently.

"I convinced them to come and help," said Mia. "Seems it wasn't worth it."

"Did you really get into the water?" asked one, eyeing them suspiciously.

"I got swept away," said Siggy.

"But what were you doing in the water in the first place?"

"Trying to swim," said Siggy.

They looked at him as if he was mad.

"Fish swim," said one. "Not us."

"But you did swim," said Mia to Alf. "I saw you."

"I had to," said Alf.

"But where did you learn? Who taught you?"

"At home, with my mum and dad."

"Your parents took you into the water," said one of the crowd. "Your parents!"

Alf nodded but kept quiet. Clearly, swimming was not a done thing on Instar.

"But what about the deep ones," asked Mia, "the ones that drag you under?"

"We don't have them where I come from," said Alf, "or at least not many. There's more danger of drowning or being struck by lightning than meeting a shark."

The Instars stared.

"They can't be from here," said one of them at last. "Maybe they're not safe."

"They're only kids," said another. "Strange, perhaps, but harmless."

"And a danger to themselves," said a man.

Mia helped remove the sticks from Alf shirt. Then she scouted around for Alf's shoes. Siggy's shoes were lost for good it seemed. One of the Instar men gave them a blanket each. He picked up Siggy and walked off quickly, as if in a hurry. Alf followed with Mia. As they went Alf saw that the beach was covered with marks and prints he could only imagine in nightmares.

Mia saw him looking. "Don't do this again," she said firmly. "Ever."

"I'll try," said Alf.

The beach was also littered with odd looking sacks. They were like burst balloons with long, delicate strands hanging down from one point. They hadn't been there the day before.

"What are those?" asked Alf.

"The silencers," said Mia. "Perhaps you saw them last night. They rise out of the sea and light the sky at this season. They mate high above the earth, then fill up with more and more gas until they explode. That's how their eggs are scattered.

Alf was fascinated. "But why call them silencers?" he asked.

"Didn't you notice?" said Mia. "When they fill the sky the darkling beasts fall silent. We think they are a blessing."

26 – Meeting

That evening there was a meeting at Nova tilting. Everyone, men, women and children, sat in the first room. It was the largest room and belonged to the whole community. Mia said it was called the Root Room because it had long underground structures like tree roots connected to its thick walls. This was the foundation for the rest of the building above it, and also what stabilized the tilting and allowed it to be so tall.

The air was tense as a large man rose and addressed the crowd.

"As Elector I have to remind you that this is the last meeting before we must decide. We cannot put it off any longer. The time approaches. In one week someone must be elevated."

"It's not fair," said a woman. She was on the verge of tears. "Why must it be a young one—and always a girl newly into womanhood. Why not elevate someone who has lived a long life, or is ill, or … " The woman stopped and sat down. Everyone looked at her sympathetically. Around her were her four daughters.

"We know, Malia; it's not easy for any of us," said the Elector.

"It's no use talking," said Mia. "Why talk? We will never decide that way. If no one volunteers we must have a drawing."

"But that's no guarantee," said another. "You know that."

"Nothing is a guarantee," said Mia fiercely. "It's a game. Choose the best three and let them draw."

There was silence. Everyone knew that she was right.

"What are they talking about?" whispered Siggy, but Alf didn't know.

"Okay," said the Elector at last. "In two days we determine the best three and let them draw. May the Great Ones help us. Let's try to remember that the chosen one is going to a better, happier life."

Everyone hung their heads.

"We also have two visitors," said the Elector, indicating Alf and Siggy. "Tell us who you are."

A sea of faces turned towards the boys. Alf and Siggy stood up. They hadn't expected to speak.

"I'm Alf," said Alf, introducing himself, "and this is Siggy. He's my friend. He used to be an ... well, never mind, he's Siggy."

"Hi," said Siggy, giving a little wave. His bright red hair was tussled and wild looking.

"Where are you from?" asked the Elector. He didn't seem too impressed with Siggy's appearance.

"Mainsfield," said Alf.

"Where's that tilting?" someone called.

"Never heard of it," called someone else.

Alf was at a loss what to answer.

"It's in another world," said Siggy. "It's dimensionally inverted. You guys are totally turned inside out—like a sock pulled the wrong way. You go through a tunnel and you're there. Bingo!"

A sea of uncomprehending faces looked back. Siggy, however, seemed pleased with his description.

The Elector was not amused. "What tilting are you from?" he asked.

Alf and Siggy stood in silence.

"They don't have a tilting," said Mia. "I'm sure of that. They came from a tunnel. I saw them."

"A tunnel," said the Elector. "No one goes underground."

"Yes, you do," said Siggy. "You dig tunnels when you're building a tilting."

"Only with permission from the Golden Ones," said the Elector, "and only by day. Even then it's dangerous. We fill them in as quickly as possible."

"We're from another world," said Alf, "but we're not beasts. You can see that."

"That's true," said Mama, speaking up. "Let's not be superstitious."

The room relaxed.

"One more night," said the Elector. "Then you go."

"But they're my guests," protested Mia.

"In *our* tilting," said the Elector. "One more night. That's it."

* * *

"What were you discussing?" asked Alf.

They were back in Mia's room. For once the air was calm and the tilting still. The light was fading fast.

"A girl, twelve or a bit older, is sent to the Golden Ones," said Mia. "They are elevated. This year our tilting has to choose one of our own."

"Does she have to go into the upper pyramid?" asked Siggy.

"Yes."

"What happens?" asked Alf.

"We're not sure. We never see them again."

"Ever?"

"No," said Mia.

Alf and Siggy were quiet for a while.

"How many ... " asked Alf.

"There are five of us in Nova tilting who qualify," said Mia. "I'm one of them."

"What if you're chosen?" asked Alf.

"I'll go," said Mia. "I must."

"What if you don't," said Siggy. "What if the tilting refuses."

"The tilting gate is torn down at night. No one will survive. It's happened before."

Alf got up and walked around the room. He was agitated. He was about to speak when Mia silenced him.

"There's nothing to discuss," she said. "We've been over it in our meetings a hundred times."

Alf looked out a window. The air was as clear as glass. Far away he caught the sparkles of the sea shining back towards him. The light was tinged with red. The sun would soon be gone. There was so much beauty in Instar, but other things as well. For a few moments the light rapidly dimmed and the green forest turned black in the reddening light. Then the utter darkness came.

* * *

The next day they followed Mia down the stairs. It was early, but she wanted to see them off at the tree before going to work.

Mama opened the gate as they left. "Don't mind the Elector," she said, patting Siggy on the shoulder.

The Darkling Beasts

The three made their way along the paths towards the big tree, then cut across the undergrowth, carefully following the blazes Siggy had made earlier. They stopped outside the entrance.

"Come with us," said Alf. "You don't have to stay."

Mia shook her head. She was afraid.

"Come on," said Siggy, taking her arm, but she still refused.

Mia raised her hand goodbye. Her eyes were moist. She turned and walked away.

Alf and Siggy dropped into the hole and entered the tunnel. They went on to the door. The sign was scraped and scratched even more.

"Let's hope it's not locked," said Alf, trying the handle. The door opened. The Hall of Mirrors was dim and quiet. Around the corner came Kitty-o.

"Kew!" she mewed, trotting eagerly towards them.

Alf picked her up. She mewed again.

"She sounds hungry," said Siggy.

They closed the door and wound their way to the entry. Outside it was still nighttime but the sky was lightening. They were back at Cam's mum's place. No wonder it was so quiet.

"The days are not the same," said Siggy. "They never quite match up."

A single bulb burned brightly at the entrance of the trailer home. It was lonely and inviting at the same time.

"Well, let's see what kind of reception we get from Cam and his mum this time," said Alf, as they walked across the dew laden grass.

27 – Ester tells

"What the flatfooted halibut do you two think you're up to?" said Cam, his unshaven face red and blotchy.

Siggy was trying not to giggle. Cam's beer belly and pink boxers made it hard to take him seriously.

"Well?" said Cam's mum, also annoyed. "What's your answer?"

"Sorry," said Alf. "There's a door in the Hall of Mirrors. We went through it."

"Course there's a door," said Cam. "There's two doors—one to go in and one to go out."

"There's a third door," said Siggy. "It's a portal."

"Portal my derriere," said Cam.

To Alf and Siggy's surprise Ester came shuffling out of the guest room. She wore a blue nightgown covered with yellow and white daisies.

"What's all the noise?" she asked, blinking in the bright kitchen light. "It's so early."

"It's them," said Cam's mum, her hands on her mountainous hips. "They've come back. Poof! Like magic! Appeared out of nowhere. Said they'd been through some portal doodle-dum in the Hall."

"The Hall is an interdimensional matrix modulator," said Siggy. "I'm sure of it. The door is just the portal. It has to do with the arrangement of mirrors, by accident or otherwise.

"How do you know that?" asked Alf.

"Sounds good," said Siggy. "But I'm right anyway."

"All's well that gets this far and no one is hurt," said Ester. "Are you boys hungry?"

Alf and Siggy nodded. Cam threw up his hands and stomped off to his room. Cam's mum and Ester began to make breakfast.

"What are you doing here?" Siggy asked Ester.

"When you vanished I said I'd come along. I told them you'd either turn up alive or never."

Cam's mum stopped suddenly. "You mean you believe them about that silly door-portal-inter ... that nonsense?"

"I do," said Ester.

"And why is that?" said Cam's mum.

"Because I came through the portal myself," said Ester. "That's how I met Jim."

Cam's mum looked thunderstruck. She began to laugh, but stopped. Lights were going on.

"That's why we never could find out where you came from," she said.

Ester nodded.

"We thought Jim was joking when he said you'd walked out of the Hall one day."

"He wasn't joking," said Ester, "though he knew you'd not believe him. It took him a long time to believe it himself."

"Where's this Jim now?" asked Alf.

"He died a couple of years ago," said Ester. " He was Cam's uncle and older than me. I lived with him for years. A perfect gentleman, he was."

"Aye, he was," said Cam's mum. "The best. But what about this other world? Is it really true?"

"Yes," said Ester. "I found the way through by accident, and came out in the Hall of Mirrors. I didn't know where I was. It was so weird. There are no mirrors in Instar. I found my way through the Hall eventually. Jim was outside the door, looking at me like he was seeing a vision." Ester rested her face in her hands for a moment. "The rest is history."

"Kew," said Kitty-o, jumping onto Ester's lap.

"What a big cat," said Ester. "Too big."

"Looks like a coon cat to us," said Cam's mum from the stove.

"No, it's not," said Alf. "She's from Instar. She has wings over there."

"Right," said Cam's mum, turning the fried eggs over, "and pigs do ballet."

28 – Materials

"What are we going to do?" asked Alf. He and Siggy were sitting with Ester in the kitchen. "Mia might be chosen. Then what?"

"It sounds like nothing has changed," said Ester. "My best friend was elected before I was. I was never happy there after that. That's why I ran."

"We have to go back and get her," said Alf. "Force her to come here if we have to."

"And if you bring her here then another young girl will have to go," said Ester.

"But at least it won't be her," said Alf fiercely.

They sat for a while.

"The beasts don't like light," said Siggy, "even the weak light of those things that floated out of the ocean—the silencers. They hid from those."

"So?" said Alf.

Siggy shrugged his shoulders. "Just thinking," he said.

The rest of the morning was spent wandering restlessly around Cam's property.

"I'm going back," said Alf.

"Me too," said Siggy. "We need food, water, flashlights and batteries—lots of batteries."

They went to Cam.

"Cam, we need flashlights," said Alf. "We're going back."

Cam grinned. "You really believe in this adventure, don't you?"

"It's real," said Siggy, looking annoyed.

"Sure," said Cam. "As real as the shoes you're wearing."

"I'm not wearing shoes," said Siggy.

"Exactly," said Cam.

"Where did we vanish then?" asked Alf.

"At the last carnival stop," said Cam. "You left while we were asleep and walked away. Easy."

"And how many miles away was the last carnival?" asked Siggy.

"Three hundred or so," said Cam.

"Right," said Siggy. "We vanish there and reappear here. And who dropped us off at five in the morning—with a huge cat too? No one. Think, Cam, think!"

Cam ran his hand over the stubble on his chin. He needed a shave; he always needed a shave. "Fine," he said at last. "I believe you," but it was clear he didn't. "So you want flashlights, do you? What kind? Pink ones or purple ones or what?"

"Bright ones," said Siggy.

"And they have to last a long time," said Alf. "All night, if need be."

"You'll need LED bulbs then," said Cam. "We'll have to go to town to get them."

"And lasers," said Siggy. "We'll need lasers."

"Like the ones the army uses for shooting down airplanes? asked Cam.

Siggy kicked him on the shin. "No," he said. "Ruby lasers, like teachers use."

Cam looked blank.

"Never mind," said Siggy. "Let's go to town."

* * *

The Darkling Beasts

Cam stopped at the thrift store first and found two flashlights. He wanted to buy Siggy a pair of shoes, but Siggy refused. He said he preferred to go barefoot from now on. He did, however, accept a new pair of jeans, a couple of shirts and a fleece jacket. They drove to the office supply store and bought batteries. They didn't have lasers.

"Try the camera store on Main Street," said the clerk.

The camera store did have lasers—red, yellow, green, blue and violet ones. Siggy wanted the yellow one. Alf chose red.

"Don't stare into them," warned the owner. "They'll damage your eyes."

Siggy wandered through the store, taking everything in. He stopped at a display cabinet full of camera flash and lighting equipment. "How much are those handheld flashes?" he asked.

"Depends," said the owner, smiling at Siggy like he was a child.

"I want a cheap but bright one," said Siggy.

"What for?" asked the owner.

"For fighting monsters in the dark," said Siggy with perfect seriousness.

The owner laughed. He turned around and rummaged in a cabinet.

"Here," he said, handing Siggy a small, clunky looking flash. "It's old and the glass is cracked, but it works a charm. I used it for years—but it doesn't fit on my new camera. It's yours—but only for fighting monsters."

Siggy's eyes opened wide. "Thank you! Thank you!" he said, pleased as punch.

"You're welcome," said the owner. "Just plug it into the wall to charge it and you're ready to go. You'll get about twenty flashes out of it. Have fun."

"And what else do my intrepid warriors need?" asked Cam after they'd left the store. "How about guns? They'd be handy."

"I wish we could," said Alf, "but no one would sell them to us."

"Have you got one?" Siggy asked Cam.

"Yes, a shotgun," said Cam, surprised at how serious they were. "So does my mum—but you can't have them."

"Pity," said Siggy.

"We'll need backpacks, too," said Alf, beginning to feel guilty at the expense.

They picked out a couple of day packs at the sports store and went home. Cam's mum made supper and Siggy ate heartily.

"Growing again?" asked Cam's mum.

"No," said Siggy. "Just stocking up. Pass the broccoli."

Siggy tucked in. Then he stopped eating. "And I'll need my shirt arms shortened."

Cam's mum raised her eyebrows. "Yes, your Highness," she said.

After supper Ester cut Siggy's wild hair. She ended up giving him a girlish pixie cut. Siggy swore that that was the last time he'd let her near him with a pair of scissors.

"Ooo, looks like we're joining the girls," said Cam, when he saw what Ester had done. "Give him lipstick."

Siggy was not amused and filched Cam's cigarette lighter when he wasn't looking.

Ester pottered around packing food into the backpacks: nuts, raisins, energy bars, sandwiches, small bottles of water.

"One more thing," said Siggy, turning to Cam. "I need a hat with a light on it. And one for Alf too."

"Like a dunces cap with a bright light on top?" asked Cam.

"Yea," said Siggy, staring him down, "just like that, only not as pointy."

Cam spent a couple of hours rigging up two old baseball caps. They had batteries, a switch, and a light on top supported with wires. They looked odd, but worked. "Don't get them wet," he warned. "I doubt they'll last in water."

Cam dug into his pocket.

"Here, take this," he said to Siggy, handing him a proper army knife. "It's better than the other."

Siggy blushed—then his eyes opened with delight. This knife had all the gear: blades, saws, screwdrivers and other gadgets.

"It's from the marines," said Cam.

"You were in the marines?" asked Alf, staring at Cam's beer belly.

"Once," said Cam, and somehow, by the way he said it, there was no more room for chatter.

* * *

Alf and Siggy spent the night in the living room. Kitty-o curled up on Alf's legs and stayed there until dawn.

At first light Siggy was up. He went to the bathroom and put on one of the new shirts Cam's mum had altered. The arms were too long because the shirt had to be bigger to accommodate his hunchback. It turned out that she'd just cut off the cuffs. Sewing wasn't her strong suit.

The boys slipped on their packs in the living room, but before they could leave Cam's mum asked them in the sweetest of tones if they'd like breakfast before they went on their expedition. She had watched the whole exercise of collecting and packing their gear with great amusement.

Ester sat with them as they ate. She didn't say much; she looked worried.

"Cam! Cam!" shouted his mum. "Get up! They're going on their safari."

Alf and Siggy ate quickly. They hadn't planned on hanging around. They put on their packs, and headed out the door. The three grownups followed them.

"Kew! Kew!" cried Kitty-o, running along beside them.

Alf climbed the steps and opened the Hall door.

"I don't know when we'll be back," he said solemnly.

Cam and his mum nodded seriously.

"Bye, then," said Siggy, and closed the door, taking Kitty-o with him.

Cam ran around the Hall of Mirrors as soon as the door closed. He came back in a few moments. He was chuckling.

"What did you do?" asked his mum.

"Blocked the other door," said Cam with a laugh. "The only way out is through this door and we'll watch it."

They retreated to the porch and settled into cheap plastic chairs. Ester made them tea as they chatted and waited. The morning sun rose strong and warm.

"I'll get them out," said Cam after an hour. "They must be bored to tears by now."

"No, no, wait," said Cam's mum. "Leave them for a while longer. Perhaps they'll come out by themselves. I can't wait to see their faces."

They waited another hour. Ester said nothing. She was half amused, but her eyes were anxious.

Finally Cam had had enough. He walked to the Hall and went inside. Five minutes later he came to the door and spread his hands. He went back inside. Cam's mum joined him. Ester stayed where she was, her gaze pensive and distant. Eventually Cam and his mum came out of the Hall and closed the door.

"They're not there," said Cam, blankly.

"So it is," said Ester, standing up and going inside the house.

29 – Gone

Alf and Siggy opened the door, flashlights in hand. The silvery walls of the passageway lit up brightly. They heard a rapid scurrying around the corner and then silence. They waited, not knowing whether to go on or not. Then Kitty-o casually sauntered ahead of them and they followed. Alf and Siggy watched in amazement as Kitty-o grew wings and shifted shape. She stopped at the opening in the tree trunk and sniffed the air, then she leapt upwards and flew away.

It was dim inside the tree trunk, but noon outside. The sun was yellow and bright.

"I can't work out the time difference," said Siggy.

"Me neither," said Alf. "I don't know whether it's a couple of hours or what."

They put their flashlights away, walked carefully over to the path, and quickly hiked to Nova tilting.

Alf knocked on the door. The peephole slid open. The eye was cold and gray.

"We're here for Mia," said Alf.

"She's gone," said a man's voice.

"Is she scraping?" asked Siggy, trying to sound friendly.

"She's gone, as in elevated," said the man. "She was chosen."

"But the chosen one didn't have to go for a week," said Alf.

"It got changed," said the man. "She went this morning," and he closed the peephole.

Alf knocked again, and again, but there was no reply. Siggy got mad and picked up a stone. He slammed it against the gate a few times.

The Darkling Beasts

The peephole flew open. "Don't do that," the man said.

"Where's Mama?" Siggy demanded.

"Scraping. Now go away."

Alf and Siggy wandered off. They were at a loss.

"We'll have to try and get her back," said Alf.

"That means getting past the guards," said Siggy. "I think we might need some stout branches."

"We're just kids," said Alf.

"All the better to take them by surprise," said Siggy, picking up a branch and whacking it against a tree to see how strong it was.

It broke.

30 – Sanctum

The pyramid loomed large. Alf couldn't help admiring it. It stood so bright and pure and tall in the sunlight. As they hiked towards it the forest paths were deserted. All those who could work were inside. As they approached the gateway in the great wall Mama walked out. She was old and bent, as if she'd aged rapidly.

"Mama," cried Siggy, running up to her.

She lifted her head. She was surprised to see them. She didn't smile and it looked as if she'd been crying. "If you came to say goodbye you're too late," she said.

"We came to get her out," said Alf.

"You'll end up dead," said Mama.

Alf and Siggy hesitated.

"We're going anyway," said Siggy. "We've brought lights, bright ones."

"And lasers," said Alf.

Mama gave them a critical look. "Lights aren't allowed here."

"Exactly," said Siggy.

"What's the best way?" asked Alf.

"There's not much to tell," said Mama. "The Golden Ones live at the top of the pyramid. Only the guards go into the sanctum—or so we are told; the doors are never opened in our presence. Generally the guards stay on Golden Hill unless there's a problem."

"But what are the Golden Ones like?" asked Alf.

"We don't know," said Mama.

"What do you mean? How can you not know?" said Siggy.

"We never see them. They never come out, not that we know of. We're not sure what they're like. The guards never say anything about them—except that they're powerful. The Teller is the only guard that passes on messages; he's the mouthpiece. Most people think the Golden Ones must be beautiful. That's their other name, The Beautiful Ones."

"Why do the guards wear those wraparound sunglasses?" asked Siggy.

"They always do," said Mama. "They never take them off, ever. And they avoid being in sunlight, they don't like it. If they have something to do outside they prefer to do it at dawn or dusk. They're vicious. Killers too. We're nothing to them."

"Wait here for us," said Alf.

"I can't," said Mama. "It's a long way back to the tilting for an old body. I can't be out at night."

She reached out and stroked Siggy on the head. Then she touched Alf. She looked at them as if she'd never see them again. She turned away and shuffled off along the path.

Alf and Siggy watched her go, then passed through the gate. The grounds were almost deserted, with only the odd person doing jobs in the fields. Some were accompanied by guard animals. One of the animals appeared beside the road and stared at the sticks in their hands, but did nothing.

As Alf and Siggy entered the pyramid two guards stopped them.

"You're late for work," said one. "It's afternoon."

"And no sticks," said the other.

"We sprained our ankles," said Siggy, suddenly lame. "It took a while to get here."

The guards faced them. Their awkward breathing was more like sniffing. There was something odd about the guards, their voices didn't ring true, as if no one was really at home. Alf felt uncomfortable. He and Siggy were out of place, especially Siggy.

"We're just kids," said Siggy, sweetly.

The guards hesitated; then grunted and jerked their heads. They could go.

The boys limped away until they were out of sight. They headed for the stairs.

The pyramid was full, the hiss of the scrapers mingling with the quiet chatter of folk talking. No one raised their voice; perhaps it was forbidden. Alf couldn't get over the size of the pyramid, it was massive. They climbed the flights of stairs one after the other without stopping. They didn't last long as their legs began to get tired.

They stopped to rest and went to a window. The light seemed suddenly bright as they approached, a splash of sunshine gleaming off the floor. They removed their backpacks and Alf let Siggy climb onto his shoulders so that he could see out. He looked over the sea of trees with the tiltings rising like impossibly thin minarets above them. Alf noticed that people had stopped working to stare at them. He tugged at Siggy's pant leg. Siggy hopped down and they returned to the stairs. They began to feel their stomachs churning. Fear was rising.

"What are we going to do?" asked Alf.

"I'm not sure," said Siggy. "We'll think of something, I hope," and he took out his camera flash and tucked it into his belt.

Alf reached into his pocket and touched his laser. He patted the side pocket of his backpack to make sure his flashlight was still there.

They came to the sanctum threshold. It was too early for most people to trade in their scrapings for food vouchers. Only a few Instars stood patiently in line while the guards weighed their boxes. Alf saw how perfect the proportions were on this floor. The architecture had certainty of craftsmanship and an understated majesty. Seven broad steps led up to the sanctum landing before the two great, ornate doors of sculptured gold. They were clearly original and untouched. All the floors below this one were plain, either by design or because they'd been scraped bare. The doors spoke with authority. Both had sun motifs, with golden rays running diagonally down the panels. Within the rays were planets and stars, and in the center, was Instar, or at least it seemed so to Alf, for there was a hollow sphere with a sun in the middle.

Alf was still staring at the doors when a guard approached.

"What are you two up to?" he barked.

The floor was suddenly quiet. Everyone stopped to see what was happening. Alf was wondering what to say when Siggy swung his staff. He hit the guard on the temple and his glasses were partly torn off his face. They dangled loosely from the side of his head.

For a moment Alf froze. The guard had no eyes, or at least not human eyes. They were bulbous and faceted, like an insect's.

A woman screamed. Siggy raised his flash and pulled the trigger. A blinding surge of light filled the golden space. The guard fell backwards onto the floor, clutching his face. All the guards did. They howled as if on fire and covered their eyes.

People scattered, desperately trying to get down the stairs. Alf and Siggy ran to the threshold doors. Alf pulled on one. It was heavy, but opened slowly.

"Quick," said Siggy. "They're getting up."

Alf pulled harder. He could hear the snorting of the guards behind him. "Okay," he cried. "In you go."

Siggy slipped through the gap and Alf followed.

The door, so slow to open, shut immediately. There was total darkness, but a strange, dry, rustling sound echoed in the space.

Alf turned on his laser. The red point of light bounced off the golden walls but didn't light the room properly. For a moment, a squat, leggy shape was seen scurrying away.

"Your flashlight," cried Alf. "Turn it on!"

Siggy was fumbling in his pack. He'd pulled the trigger of the flash, but it was still recharging. He found his flashlight and flipped the switch. Loud hisses erupted and a frantic scurrying of feet. They saw insects, like cockroaches, big ones, golden brown and ugly. They were huge—larger than dogs, and wide and squat. The place suddenly filled with a stinking, musty, suffocating odor as the insects frantically scrambled over each other to get away from the light.

Alf retched and put his hand to his mouth. Then he fumbled for his flashlight too. "Let's go," he said, turning it on. "We don't know how long we have."

They crossed the room. Golden bowls sat on the floor in a line. They had gold dust in them. Some had overturned in the mad scramble to get out. It looked like the cockroaches had been feeding from them. Two passages, one left and one right, led out of the room.

"Which one?" asked Alf.

"If we wait it might not matter," said Siggy, turning around.

The doors behind them were opening. Siggy ran to them, raised his flash and pulled the trigger. The guards roared in the intense light and fell back. The doors shut again.

"Let's go," said Alf, running for the right hand passage.

They passed through the archway and down a hall. The walls were covered with sculpted reliefs and patterns. They came to a doorway on the left and looked in. Two cockroaches hissed and emitted a high-pitched screech. They charged at the boys, knocking them over as they clambered to get away.

Alf and Siggy got up. They were smeared with a foul smelling liquid.

"Ugg," said Siggy. "Cockroach juice."

Alf tried to say something but bent over and vomited. He retched until his stomach was empty.

Siggy shone his flashlight around the room. The walls were ornately decorated but the room was filled with a pile of pellets, as if the cockroaches did their business there. Each pellet was the size of a small fist.

Alf finished throwing up and wiped his mouth. They went further. There were more rooms along the passageway, but now they shone their lights into the room from a distance and flushed out any roaches hiding inside. Every room was piled high with golden pellets which spilled out into the halls.

They found a stairway. It was narrow and steep with tall steps and high headroom. They climbed up. Again two passages, one left and one right. The air was thick and foul. They could hear the cockroaches fleeing ahead of them or finding ways to get around them via other passages.

They climbed several flights of stairs and wound through the halls. The rooms on each floor were filled to overflowing with golden slugs and pellets. Finally they found a room with normal food and water sitting on a table. Then they hurried on. They mounted a narrow flight of stairs that led to a single room. They were almost at the apex, the sloping sides of the pyramid making up the four walls. An ornate, ladder-like stairway led upward to what must be the final room.

From one corner came a whimper. It was Mia, shielding her eyes from the light. She was chained by the waist to the wall.

Alf ran over. "Mia! Are you okay?"

"It's up there," she said, ignoring his question. "Up the ladder."

Alf turned. Two long antennae were vibrating and beating against the upper opening. Siggy was in the middle of the room gazing upwards, a look of disgust on his face. The head appeared. It was a massive roach. The creature moved with incredible rapidity. It scuttled half way down the ladder and launched itself at Siggy. Alf was shocked at its size—twice that of the others, and longer and slimmer. Siggy toppled backwards and screamed as the insect hit him. At the same moment a brilliant flash of light lit the room. Alf saw that the cockroach was golden, completely. It hissed as it scrambled off Siggy and backed away. Alf swore he heard words in the hissing. Siggy lay motionless on the floor. Alf pointed his laser at the creature. Its compound eyes were as big as grapefruit and he focused the beam on one of them. Instantly the insect let out a high-pitched squeal. It leaped backwards and tumbled down the stairs. It scurried away, a stream of hissed invective trailing off into silence.

Alf ran to Siggy.

"My head hurts," Siggy groaned. A cut over his eye poured blood down his face.

"You'll be alright," said Alf, picking him up and hoping he was speaking the truth. "We have to get Mia."

Mia was struggling to get free. She was chained to the wall with a cable spun from thick strands of gold. The cable flared out around her body and squeezed her waist. "It's no use," she said. "I can't get free."

"The saw," said Alf. "In your army knife."

Siggy pulled out the knife and opened the saw blade. The golden strands slowly wore away. One snapped, then two. In a moment he was sweating profusely in the thick air and his hands became slippery.

"Your turn," he said when he started to slow, and Alf took over.

Siggy stepped back and looked at Mia. She was a mess, and stank. Her clothes were ripped and covered with stains, as if she'd fought with the insect. She didn't look at him, but kept her gaze on the cable where Alf was sawing, as if that was all that mattered.

The Darkling Beasts

Siggy looked around. The other corners of the room had cables coming from the wall too. One of them had a pile of old tattered clothes with white bones lying randomly here and there. A skull lay on its side, its eyes gazing vacantly into space.

Siggy climbed the ornate ladder and cautiously shone his flashlight around the space. It was the topmost room in the pyramid, it's peaked ceiling rising to a point. At the apex was a partial sphere, and sun rays ran down the wall and ended in flames. The space immediately in front of the ladder was clear, the floor crowded with inlaid stars of many kinds. They were made of crystal and sparkled in the light.

Siggy entered. A low wall surrounded the opening in the floor on three sides. Everywhere else was filled with golden cockroach pellets, heaps and heaps of them. Against the back wall was a rectangular block, like an altar. It too had a sun motif. On top of the altar was a chaotic nest of torn fabric, sticks and slime. This was the creatures nest.

Siggy went back down. Mia had taken over and was sawing at the cable with all the strength of desperation.

"Almost there," said Alf.

Finally the cable broke. Mia still had the waistband on, but at least she was free.

"Let's go," said Alf, and they headed for the stairs.

31 – Escape

The three made their way through the upper pyramid. They heard scuttling around them, but only twice caught a fleeting glimpse of a roach scurrying away. Metal slugs lay scattered everywhere, knocked out of the rooms by the insects in their haste. Alf picked one up. It was heavy and dense. He put a few into his pockets. They might come in handy as weapons.

"We're near where we came in," said Siggy, after a while.

At the bottom of the final stairs a guard lay stretched out. His throat had been cut, but there was hardly any blood. His body looked deflated, as if sucked empty. They went on cautiously, winding in and out of the maze-like passages. Soon the entry room lay ahead. They heard guttural voices.

"Guards," whispered Mia, halting.

The voices stopped speaking.

"Turn off the lights," said Siggy.

In a moment they were in complete darkness.

"They have the advantage in the dark," whispered Alf.

"Shhh," said Siggy. "Listen!"

Alf listened. He hardly dared to breathe. He heard faint steps, scratchings and rustlings, but also breathing. The guards couldn't hide their breathing. They were coming towards them. Alf gripped his flashlight and took a gold slug from his pocket.

"Now!" screamed Siggy, and his flash burst into white light. Alf saw three guards a few feet down the passage. He hurled a slug and hit one square in the face. The guard staggered back, roaring in pain.

"Go! Go!" shouted Mia.

The three ran towards the guards, waving their flashlights and lasers and shouting wildly. The guards turned and fled before them. They flung their weight against the great doors and they flew open. The three were on their heels. They stopped on the landing. The tables and chairs were overturned. Gold dust, boxes and weighing scales lay scattered on the floor. The pounding of the guard's boots echoed through the building as they fled down the stairs.

"We have to get out," said Mia urgently.

Down the endless stairs they went. Suddenly they saw a body. It was one of the people. Mia stopped and put her hand on his heart. She shook her head. She turned him over. There was a neat hole in the back of his neck. They went on. They saw more bodies, all dead. The guards must have killed people in their panic. Possessions lay scattered about. It was utter chaos.

They fled the pyramid and down the avenue. The whole place was deserted. Not a soul was in sight and they wondered where all the guards had gone. A guard animal appeared out of the vegetation and ran towards them.

"Stop," cried Mia, and they halted.

The animal slowed down and eyed them intently.

"Walk slowly," said Mia. "Don't look at it. Pretend to chat. If it attacks, watch your throat and fight to the death, they never give up."

The Darkling Beasts

They went on, casually walking forwards and trying not to look at the animal.

"Nice weather," said Siggy.

"Lovely," said Alf. "It must be half-past four."

"Time for tea," said Siggy. "Tea and muffins—blueberry muffins with honey and slathers of butter melting in your mouth."

Alf and Mia laughed—a genuine laugh.

"Trust Siggy to talk about food," said Alf.

The guard animal suddenly turned and walked away.

"Keep chatting," said Mia, and so they did until they reached the gate. Then they took off as if the devil himself was behind them.

32 – Truth

"What do we do now?" asked Siggy.

They were sitting on a forest path near Nova tilting. It peeked through the trees not far away.

"Mia should come back with us," said Alf. "Then we'd all be safe."

Mia hung her head. "What about the rest of my tilting? They won't be safe."

"What will those guards and bugs do now?" asked Siggy.

"I don't know," said Mia. "I'm the only one to have returned. We all thought the Golden Ones were refined and cultured."

"You really didn't know?" said Alf.

"No," said Mia. "The myth was that they were beautiful, that they'd built the Golden Pyramid; then lived in it out of sight because they were too lovely to behold."

"And that's it?" asked Siggy.

"Well, I shortened the tale," said Mia, "but in essence, that's it."

"And you believed it?"

"Yes," said Mia, "why not?"

Mia pushed back her hair. Her face was streaked with slime.

"But there was another story," she said nervously, "one that was only whispered at night."

"Go on," said Siggy.

"It said that most of the Golden Ones had departed, but a few stayed on to direct and advise. At first things had gone on as before. As time passed the line of the Golden Ones weakened and the leader had to take a normal person for a husband. She conferred her title to her children when she died, but the children became greedy. They dug further into the earth to get more gold. That's when the underworld was opened. That's when the Golden Ones stopped being seen."

"That tale is closer to the truth," said Alf. He looked at the sky. The afternoon was getting old and the sun dimming. "We can't just sit here, we have to move on."

"I'm going to my tilting," said Mia, standing up and walking away.

Alf and Siggy grabbed their backpacks and followed. In a few minutes they stood outside the gate. Mia knocked and the peephole slid open. An eye stared at her. It was fearful.

"It's me, Jonin," said Mia. "Open up."

"You're not supposed to be here," said Jonin.

"Well, I am. Now open the door."

"I can't let you in. The tilting might be destroyed."

"It might be destroyed anyway," said Mia.

Jonin hesitated. "Wait," he said at last.

A bell rang three times and people streamed out of their rooms. A few minutes later the gate opened and the tiltings came out. There must have been two hundred of them, children included. They made a circle around the threesome. No one came close. They eyed Mia's dirty clothes and golden waistband, not knowing what to make of it. Last of all Mama hobbled out. She walked directly up to Mia and gave her a hug. She had tears in her eyes.

"What do you want?" asked the Elector, stepping forward.

"I want to come home," said Mia.

"Then we'll all die," said the Elector. "You know this. The Golden Ones will destroy us."

"There are no Golden Ones," said Siggy.

There was shocked silence.

"Of course there are," said the Elector. "We all know that."

"No, there's not," said Alf. "We've been inside. Ask Mia."

All eyes turned to her.

"There are no Golden Ones," said Mia. "Just large roaches, and a king roach. There must be a queen somewhere in there too."

People stared. It didn't make sense to them and doubt played across their faces.

"What about the guards?" asked a woman.

"They're controlled," said Mia. "They're half breeds as far as I can tell."

"And why were you brought there?" asked the Elector.

"For breeding," said Mia. "Like I said, the guards are half breeds."

She said it so flatly that there was no doubting her word. The shock at what she was saying was palpable.

"Did they ... ?" asked Mama, a fierce look on her face.

"No," said Mia. "I fought the king off. Look at my clothes. But it was only a matter of time before I become too weak, or gave up. Then the King would have bred me." The loathing in her voice was hard to listen to.

"What about the others," asked the Elector, "the others that were elevated?"

"Dead," said Mia. "Eaten, once they were used."

There was complete silence. After a moment a couple of children started to cry and their mothers led them away. Soon others followed.

"You're lying," said a man.

"No, she isn't," said Alf fiercely. "We saw it too. Just look at her—why would the Golden Ones smear her with stench and chain her to a wall," and he grabbed the cable around Mia's waist and held it up.

"She is telling the truth," said Mama.

Mama's statement was not as an argument. She said it as a simple fact. It was clear that her words held weight.

"And if it is true, what are we supposed to do about it?" asked the Elector.

"Fight," said Siggy fiercely.

It sounded strange coming from such a small body. A few people couldn't help smiling.

"How?" asked a man called Jhek. "I'd fight if I'm shown how. After they elevated my daughter my life became worthless. If she's dead, I'd be happy to die fighting them."

"Wait a minute," said the Elector. "We have to discuss this. It's not so simple."

"It is simple," said Siggy. "Fight or die. Period. Time marches; the sun moves to its closing."

Alf rolled his eyes and wondered where Siggy got some of his phrases.

33 – First Battle

The sun was fading quickly. Darkness was not far off. The air felt heavy, as if a thunderstorm was on the way. Alf noticed that many in the crowd were sweating. They were terrified, yet trying not to show it. The discussion jerked back and forth. Some were clear that there was no choice; others retreated into wishes and hopes. Finally a group of women grabbed their children and broke away.

"We're going to another tilting," they said. "We can't just stay and let our children die."

"Don't," said Mama. "The other tiltings won't let you in. They'll say you'll contaminate them."

"We're not an illness," one shouted. "Some of them have been friends for years."

"Friends enough to risk their children for you?" asked Mama. She shook her head. "No, they won't let you in."

A few saw that she made sense and stayed. Others left, hurrying away into the dimming forest.

"What weapons do you have?" asked Alf.

"None," the men said. "They're not allowed."

"Have you got knives? Spears? Guns?" asked Siggy.

"What are guns?" they asked. "And no, we don't have any knives at the tiltings. They're not allowed."

"Then gather stones," said Alf. "And stout sticks."

"We could use the shovels and picks," said Mia, running off towards a shed leaning against the outer wall.

Men and women ran into the forest to gather sticks and stout staves, others gathered stones—though there weren't many to be had; the soil was mostly clay. Alf and Siggy helped Mia get the digging tools from the shed.

"How about fire?" asked Siggy. "We could build a fire in the courtyard. The beasts are afraid of light."

"We don't know how to make fire," said Mia. "They're not allowed. If lightning strikes and the forest burns we have to stay in our tiltings until it's over."

Siggy immediately ran out the gate. "Bring dry branches too," he shouted. "As many as you can."

They managed to collect enough wood for one bonfire before the light faded. The gates clanged shut as the last spark of sun vanished. Alf couldn't get used to how quickly it became dark. When the sun was gone nothing but darkness reigned. He turned on his flashlight. People gasped when they saw it and gathered around. They'd never seen light being used this way. Alf put his cap on Mia and showed her how to turn the bulb on and off. "Don't use it unless you really have to," he said. "It only lasts for a while. And don't knock it around either," he added, "it's delicate."

Siggy turned on his flashlight as well. Now there were three pools of light playing in the courtyard. They were small in comparison to the surroundings, but comforting.

"When they attack, how do they get in?" asked Siggy.

"We don't know," said Jhek.

"What do you mean you don't know?" asked Siggy, astonished.

"There are hardly ever any survivors," said Jhek, "and besides, they come in the dark when we cannot see. All we know is that the gates are torn off their hinges and the people dead. Many are eaten, or their blood drained."

From outside the wall the night cries were beginning.

Alf looked around, shining his flashlight from face to face.

"Where's the Elector?"

No one had seen him for a while.

"I saw him go towards the pyramid when we were gathering wood," said a young girl.

Alf knew there wasn't time to worry about him. It was time to act.

"Mia, you come with me. Siggy, give me your laser and guard the gate with your camera flash. Jhek, make a pile of wood near the gate.

Alf ran up the tilting stairs with Mia behind him until they could see over the wall. He shone his flashlight into the forest. Instantly that part of the forest exploded with cries. Vague shapes fled away. Then silence—or at least silence in the immediate neighborhood, for further away the howling and throbbing continued.

Alf was disappointed with his flashlight. The forest was too far away and only general shapes and shadows could be seen. He climbed further up the tilting. As he shone his light into a new part of the forest there would be a hue and cry and shapes fleeing away, but on the other side of the tilting, where it was dark, the night sounds had already started up again.

Alf turned on Siggy's laser and gave it to Mia. "Don't look into it, or shine it in other people's eyes," he warned, turning on his own.

Mia was fascinated. They shone their beams into the forest. They carried a long way, out beyond their ability to see, but they only made a small circle of light.

"Let's find one of these thingies that go bump in the night," said Alf.

He told Mia to follow his beam with hers. He turned off his flashlight and his eye's adjusted as he scanned the tree tops with his laser. He caught a glimmer; something reflected back to him.

"There," he said, holding his light steady. "What's that?"

Mia's light beam joined his. For an instant they caught two gleams staring back at them from high in the canopy. Then whatever it was screamed and leaped backwards and went tumbling to the ground. There was silence in that sector for a while.

"Perhaps we can keep them away for one night," said Alf. "I hope we have enough battery power to last till the morning."

"What are batteries?" asked Mia.

Alf was about to explain when the crowd in the tilting yard roared in fear.

Alf and Mia ran down the stairs in time to see Siggy standing in the open, tiny and all alone. On his head was the silly looking cap with a small bulb on top. Before him rose the double doors of the gate. Over the gate a creature of darkness was crawling. It was indistinct in the poor light, but it emanated a raw, visceral menace.

The Darkling Beasts

The tiltings had withdrawn back into the shadows, as if hiding in the darkness would protect them from this thing. They crouched, crawled, groaned on all fours or lay faint on the ground.

Siggy screamed: high pitched, childish, defiant, courageous in the face of all his fears. He ran towards the beast and let off his flash. Alf saw the creature fall backwards. There was a dull thud, then all he heard was Siggy cursing wildly.

Alf ran to him. Siggy was shouting invectives in a language he'd never spoken before. Siggy was so intense that Alf had a hard time getting him to stop.

"Siggy! Siggy! It's gone," he said. "Stop shouting."

"You piece of tessalated excrement," screamed Siggy. "I know what realms you inhabit. I know, and I defy them!"

Siggy marched away from Alf. His blood was up.

"Fire!" he shouted. "Light the fire!"

"We don't know how," said Jhek, stepping into the light.

This simple statement stopped Siggy in his tracks and brought him to his senses.

"Easy," he said, taking out Cam's lighter. He walked over and lit the wood beside the gate. Soon a fire blazed, bathing the tilting in warm hues all the way to the top.

The tiltings gathered around and stared at the flames. The night sounds in the immediate vicinity died away altogether. Alf and Siggy set up lookouts in four directions on the tilting stairs. The night wore on. They stoked the fire and changed batteries now and then. Later they heard rustling in the forest, like large insects; also the paper-dry flapping of wings, but they saw nothing.

Finally the sun appeared. At first it was only a pin head and weak, but in the strengthening light of the world the tiltings went into their homes or the common room and slept where they lay down.

34 – Farlin

Alf woke Siggy. He was sound asleep beside what was left of the fire. He looked dirty and pathetic. The cut over his eye had dried dark brown.

"We have to go," said Alf. "Our batteries won't last another night."

Siggy rubbed his eyes. His hair looked like a madman's holiday.

"I suppose," he said groggily.

The gate opened and Jhek came over with a stranger.

"This is Farlin," he said. "He's from another tilting."

Farlin looked at the two boys—especially Siggy. Amusement flickered crossed his face, but not for long.

"The guards have closed the pyramid grounds," he said. "No one can work. We'll soon be without food."

"The other tiltings are saying it's our fault," added Jhek. "They say we shouldn't have taken you in."

"So the other tiltings don't mind giving their young women away?" asked Alf.

"No, but … " said Farlin.

"No, but yes, or no, but no?" asked Siggy.

"We can't break the law," said Farlin.

"Cruelty is no law," said Siggy.

"What are you going to do?" asked Jhek.

"We want these two to leave," said Farlin, indicating the boys.

"And the guards and their cockroach king will let everything get back to normal?" asked Alf.

"Perhaps," said Farlin, rubbing his foot on the ground. "And we don't believe the Golden Ones are roaches. That's impossible. They're too wealthy and wise."

Mia came down from the tilting and walked over. Her golden waistband had been cut off and she'd washed and changed into a fresh dress. Her old dress was in one hand. She heard what Farlin said.

"The Golden Ones are vermin," said Mia. "I was there. I was 'elevated'. I saw the king. He crawled all over me. Smell," and she pushed her dress into Farlin's face.

He jerked back, disgusted.

"That's your Golden One," said Mia, throwing her dress onto the remnants of the bonfire.

"We are going to fight," Jhek said to Farlin. "We have no choice. We all expect to die anyway."

A wail of sorrow rose from the gate. Mia went over and immediately came back.

"They found the bodies of the women and children who left last night—or at least what was left of them. They got to Seavell's tilting but they wouldn't let them in."

"How many will have to die before you fight?" Alf asked Farlin. "Join us."

Farlin nodded. His mind was made up. "I'll see what I can do," he said. "I know others are tired of having their children taken. I'll be back, if I can."

"Wait," said Siggy, and he fished in his pack. He brought out a long kitchen knife and handed it to him. He'd borrowed it from Cam's mum, hoping she wouldn't mind. "Take this with you. You might meet guards."

"Thanks," said Farlin, testing the blade. It was dull. "The guards are nowhere in sight. Not for long, I suppose," and he strode off rapidly.

"We have to go," said Alf to Mia.

"No, we need you," said Mia, shocked that they would leave so soon.

"Our batteries will run out in a few hours," said Alf. "It's better if we use the time to get more."

Alf and Siggy gave out what equipment they could to Jhek and Mia. They kept their packs and a golden roach pellet.

"Gather lots of firewood," said Siggy, "as much as you can. Burn it bright, and use the flashlights and lasers as little as possible."

"Won't you get back by tonight?" asked Mia.

"We'll try," said Alf. "But our times are offset, we're not sure if it's day or night over there."

They put on their packs and passed through the gate. The day-star was warming and golden. Alf looked back to see Mia standing on the tilting stairs, her soft hair framing her face. She looked wistfully after them. Then they hiked up the path through the forest towards the hollow tree.

35 – Slug of Gold

As soon as the door closed behind them the Hall of Mirrors began to shake.

"What the bean!" exclaimed Siggy. "What's happening?"

Alf steadied himself against a wall. For a moment he thought they'd walked into an earthquake. Then he laughed.

"Cam's driving somewhere," he said. "We're on the road."

Siggy grinned. "I didn't know what was happening for a moment."

They made their way to the entrance. It was locked. So was the exit. The two small skylights gave what little light there was so they sat under one and waited. An hour passed. Then two.

"Where's he going?" said Siggy, getting fed up.

Another hour passed and still they were on the road. It was a freeway, for they only heard cars and trucks overtake them. Alf banged on the wall nearest the cab and shouted, but more out of boredom than any expectation of being heard.

Another hour passed and they were still going. Alf was getting antsy. There was lots to do. They'd entered a hilly landscape, the truck slowing down and laboring and then speeding up again.

"Does the man not pee?" asked Siggy. "And if he doesn't, I do."

Finally they pulled off the main road and turned right and left a number of times. Then they stopped.

"Cam! Cam!" shouted Alf and Siggy, banging on the exit. "Open the door!"

Key's rattled and the door swung open. A complete stranger stood staring at them.

"Where's Cam?" asked Alf.

"Who the hell are you?" said the man.

"I'm Alf. This is Siggy. Where's Cam?"

The man looked back and forth between them.

"How did you get in there? I looked good before I left. Cam said to, in case there wer'd a cat."

Siggy shrugged. "You must have missed us."

The man didn't believe him.

"What's with your back?" he asked. "Looks hunched or summin'—and your head's cut."

Siggy didn't reply. He jumped out of the doorway and marched off to look for a toilet. Alf hopped down. The man closed the door and locked it. They were at another carnival venue, this one in a field on the edge of a town.

"Where's Cam?" Alf asked again.

"He coming," said the man. "His mum had to go to the doctor. She'll come tomorrow."

"Kew!" came a plaintive cry from inside the Hall.

"It's Kitty-o," said Alf, going back to the door. "Open it, please ... what's your name?"

"Harry," the man said, unlocking the door.

Out jumped Kitty-o. She ignored Alf and Harry and took off after Siggy.

"Now I'm flummoxed," said Harry. "You didn't know about that cat either, did you? You just spent hours in there. What's happening?"

"We must have missed her," said Alf, running after Siggy and leaving Harry to stare after him.

The boys wandered through the carnival. Alf had cleaned up Siggy's head. Already the wound was almost healed—because he had decided to fix it, Siggy claimed. A few vendors recognized them and waved hello. Some wanted to pet Kitty-o. They looked for Ester, but she wasn't there. No one knew if she was coming or not. Finally Cam came rattling along in his mum's rig and pulled up next to the Hall. He sat in the cab and looked at Alf and Siggy.

"Don't say you're not happy to see us," said Siggy.

Cam pushed back his cap and spit out the window. He was chewing sunflower seeds.

"You came back," he said at last. "I suppose you're hungry."

"Give us a break," said Siggy. "We haven't eaten for ages."

Cam tossed Siggy a sandwich and he began to wolf it down.

"Been growing again, have you?" said Cam, getting out of the cab.

"No," said Siggy, sulkily.

Alf and Siggy followed Cam around as he set up his mum's stall.

"We have to get more flashlights and batteries," said Alf. "Now. There's no time to spare."

"And a generator," said Siggy. "Plus gas and halogen floodlights."

"Sure, sure," said Cam, securing the awning. "How about an eighteen wheel tractor-trailer to carry all the gear?"

"It's serious," said Alf, grabbing Cam's arm. "People are dying."

Cam finished putting the awning into place. He stood and faced them.

"Listen," he said. "I know about dying. I've been in a war. I'd love to help, but I'm not a bank. A few more batteries and a flashlight or two and that's it. My mum's sick, and Harry over there is not working for nothing. When I'm done we'll go, and the quicker you leave me alone the quicker I'll be," and he went back to setting things up.

The boys sat on the Hall stairs. They were down in the mouth and didn't know what to do. Finally Cam finished and sauntered over.

"Let's go," he said.

Alf and Siggy grabbed their packs.

"You won't need those," said Cam. "Give them to me and I'll lock them in the truck."

He took them and swung them onto the seat.

"What have you got in there?" he asked, patting one with his hand. "Been collecting rocks, have you?"

He opened a pocket and took out the golden slug.

"What in the name of naugahyde is this?" he said, hefting the shiny slug in his hand.

"It's a giant cockroach's doo-doo," said Siggy.

"And I'm the President's poodle dog," said Cam, holding the slug to the light. "This looks like gold."

"It is," said Alf. "I'd forgotten. It might be worth something."

"You'd forgotten?" said Cam, unbelieving.

"We've been trying to tell you the important part," said Alf.

"You never mentioned nothing about gold," said Cam, suddenly interested in their adventure. He hefted the slug, feeling its weight. "How many have you got here?"

"Just one."

"I know the very man who might give us a few smooth quick-boys for this," said Cam. "Let's go."

Cam told Harry to keep an eye on things and they made their way into the town. It was old and sat on a steep hill. Many of the buildings were half stone and half wood. Not a few leaned to the left or right, or loomed precariously over the narrow streets.

"What place is this?" asked Siggy.

"Wendover," said Cam. "It's old, as you can see. It used to be a fort town. It's built in the English style and named after a town in York. Some of the inhabitants came over in the days when the Wellybygs were plundering for fat cattle and a wife."

They climbed two twisting flights of stairs with a mixture of shops and private houses on either side. Near the top of the second stairs a store sign hung low over their heads: 'SAGWARTS: BROKER TO KINGS SINCE 1095' it said in Gothic script.

"What's that supposed to mean?" asked Alf.

"King Wendstael of Great Britain was on the march and fell short of cash to pay his troops," said Cam, "or so the legend goes. The King went into a pawnbroker to get some ready cash. The owner, Old Sagwart, refused to hand any over unless the King gave a surety."

'You look like a King and you might even be a King,' said Old Sagwart, 'but gold is gold and stays precious no matter who is King. I need a surety.'

"King Wendstael, rather than being offended, laughed and pulled off a jeweled ring from his finger and handed it over. After that Old Sagwart changed the sign. A direct descendent came to America and brought the sign with him and the tradition carried on. Old Andy inside is the last in the line. When he goes the tale comes to an end."

They entered and a bell tinkled over their heads. The place was packed from floor to ceiling with every imaginable object: desks, clothes, books, vacuums, a wood stove, decoy ducks, carpets, bicycles and a real penny farthing with a big price tag.

"Andy! Andy!" called Cam. "Where are you, you old sod?"

An old man appeared out of the back of the shop. He wore a collarless, workingman's shirt and a striped suit vest.

"Cam! Dude! Welcome!" he cried, throwing up his arms. "A pleasure to see ya!"

"Andy, this here is Alf, and his friend Siggy," said Cam, introducing them.

"Ah, a hunchback," said Andy, peering at Siggy's back. "Poor lad," and he patted Siggy on the head.

Siggy swiped his hand away. "I'm not," he said, venomously. "I'm an incarnated elf."

"That's right, lad," said Andy with a chuckle, "and I'm a leprechaun from Fiddler's Green. Now, what can I do for ya?"

Cam held out the gold slug. Andy took it up, his eyes widening in wonder.

"Now that's a nugget," he said, turning it over and feeling its weight. He took it to the counter and put it on his scales. He did a few more tests.

"Four pounds, 6 ounces," he said, "and pure. Worth a pretty buck or two."

"How much" asked Alf.

"I'll give you seven hundred smooth boys straight up," said Andy. "No questions asked."

"Seven hundred!" exclaimed Cam.

"Eight hundred, then," said Andy, giving Cam a dirty look.

Eight hundred!" cried Alf and Siggy together. This was beyond anything they'd imagined.

"Fine, a thousand," said Andy, reluctantly. "And not a finkle more, or you'll have me bankrupt."

"Done," said Cam, not believing his ears, and he shot a look at the boys to keep them quiet.

Andy had to dig into a few hiding places to come up with the cash.

"Where did you get this lump?" he asked. "I've never seen the like of it."

"A parallel dimension," said Siggy. "It's cockroach droppings."

"Fine, fine," said Andy, looking annoyed. "Don't tell me then."

36 – Stymie

Cam bought himself a backpack, a big one. They loaded up with food, batteries, lasers, large flashlights with powerful beams, cigarette lighters and handheld flash packs for cameras. They went to the sports store and bought target bows and arrows. Cam bought a brightly colored flare gun and distress flares. Then he found a pricey hunter's camouflage outfit and got it too. He put it on straight away and admired himself in the mirror.

"You can't go hunting with them target bows," said the shop owner, looking at Cam in his new outfit. "'Gainst the law."

"No, no, we're not," said Cam, blushing. "This outfit's for later in the year, and the bows are for the boys."

Cam cut an unlikely figure in his shiny new gear as they browsed the local hardware store. The price tag was still sticking out the neck. They bought a box of fire starters and Siggy found machetes for clearing brush.

"Well, well," said Harry when they appeared back at the carnival. "I see that the revolution is about to begin. Long live the Reign of King Cam and the Boys!"

"Very funny," said Cam, and then told Harry that he was leaving.

"But what about the Hall of Mirrors?" said Harry. "What will happen to it when you're gone?"

"Never mind," said Cam. "If anyone asks, say I'm sick. If I'm not back when the carnival is over, pay someone to drive the rig home," and he handed Harry a wad of twenties.

Cam followed Alf and Siggy through the labyrinth of mirrors. Round and round they went until they reached the door—but the door was not there. Even the passage leading up to it was missing.

"Drat," said Siggy. "I knew it would happen sometime."

"Come on, guys," said Cam. "Where's this door you've been telling me about?"

"It's usually here," said Alf, "but sometimes it's gone. It has to be—otherwise you'd have found it years ago."

"Right," said Cam. "What a fool I've been. Spending all that good money too. For a while I believed you."

"But it's true," said Siggy. "Where do you imagine we've been appearing and disappearing from?" but Cam was having none of it and he marched out of the Hall.

"Back already from the great expedition?" said Harry when Cam appeared. "Thought you'd be gone for at least an hour or two."

Cam said nothing. He climbed into the truck cab and slammed the door so hard the whole rig shook.

Alf and Siggy stayed in the Hall. There was nothing to do but wait, and wait they did, for hours. The day, late already when they came into the Hall, ended, and twilight fell. The sound of the gathering carnival crowd was muffled and dim. Cam didn't bother opening the Hall; he was in the pub drinking. They must have dozed off because one minute they were talking and the next it was completely dark and Stumpy was pawing them.

Siggy turned on a flashlight. The door was there again.

"Hi, Stumpy," he said, stroking his back.

Siggy's hand immediately felt wet. He pointed his flashlight. There was blood. Stumpy's shoulder was gashed.

"There's been fighting," said Alf, jumping up. "We have to go—now!"

He pushed the door open and in a moment they were climbing into the hollow tree.

37 – Skirmish

Alf and Siggy cautiously stepped out of the hollow tree into the forest. It was night. It felt late at night, though it was hard to say why. The darkness seemed tired, or perhaps it was the moist smell of dew on the leaves. Their flashlights pierced the darkness like daggers and an unseen creature fled through the underbrush. Shouts were coming from Nova tilting. They followed Siggy's blaze marks to the path and began to run, their gear bouncing up and down and hindering their stride.

The tilting came into view. For a moment they thought it was burning. Flames behind the wall were leaping skyward and lighting the whole façade. Howls and dry clicks greeted Alf and Siggy as they approached the

The Darkling Beasts

open space in front of the gate. Dark shapes fled their probing lights and the forest around them was alive with crawling things.

"Let's use our camera flashes," said Alf, and they let them off one after the other. In the open space they were not as powerful as indoors, but for two moments the whole scene lit up. Guards were there, in amongst the trees. So too were cockroaches. Some had wings extended as they scurried to get way. Other, darker shapes, howled at the light but couldn't be properly seen.

Something hard hit Alf on the shoulder. He dropped his camera flash and the bulb shattered.

"Watch out!" he cried. "They're throwing things."

He fumbled to get a second flashlight from his pack. As he turned it on he caught a glimpse of a golden ball on the ground. That's what had hit him. Another grazed his leg and went skittering along the ground. Then Siggy was hit in the chest with a dull thud. Alf yelled as Siggy collapsed.

Wings, dry insect wings, fluttered and beat the air around them. Alf scanned the sky. The cockroaches were flying. They were dropping metal slugs from a great height. It was deadly. They hit the ground like metal rain.

Alf grabbed Siggy and dragged him against the trunk of a large tree. Here they were mostly sheltered. Siggy was panting heavily. The wind had been knocked out of him.

"Use the bow," he gasped. "I'll hold the light."

Alf handed a flashlight to Siggy, slipped off his bow and fitted an arrow. Siggy lit up a flying cockroach and Alf let the arrow fly. The cockroach fell from the air with a high-pitched screech. It hit the ground with a crunch and tried to crawl away, but couldn't.

"One down," said Alf, fitting another arrow.

Slugs began to pound against the tree trunk behind them. Siggy searched with the flashlight. Someone was throwing them from the cover of the trees. One hit Alf on the head and he fell to his knees. Blood gushed into his eyes. He was dazed and struggled to find his feet.

"Guards," shouted Siggy, pointing the light.

Alf staggered up and let an arrow fly. It caught a guard in the throat. He gurgled and flailed before falling over. The rest retreated into the forest.

Suddenly, firebrands flew over the tilting wall. They burnt brightly on the ground, illumining the whole space. The gate flew open. Mia stood there with a flaming branch in her hands.

"Alf—Siggy—run!" she cried.

The boys whipped out their machetes and ran. Slugs thudded on the ground around them. One hit Siggy on his backpack. It twisted him around and he fell. An instant later something reached out of the ground and grabbed his foot. Alf stopped. A huge, grub-like creature had appeared from under the leaf litter and was dragging Siggy underground. Alf hacked at it with his machete. Its head was hard and the blade glanced off. He hacked again behind the head and the blade sliced through. The creature grunted and pulled away, leaving a trail of slime.

"Get out of here!" Alf shouted.

They made a mad scramble for the gate, plunged through and Mia slammed the bolts shut.

In the courtyard a huge fire burned. The ground was littered with golden slugs. A few bodies lay crumpled here and there, and a huge cockroach was half burned in the fire. It stank like smoldering hair.

Jhek came running from the tower, holding a table as a shield above his head. "Well done, lads. You gave them hell."

"They gave us hell too," said Siggy, rubbing his chest.

Jhek and Mia ran with them to the tilting as metal rain thundered on the ground around them. They reached the common room and in moments the sky was alight with laser rays and flashlights. The beams danced off the trees, probing into the darkness and forcing the guards and flying cockroaches away.

38 – *Morning*

Alf and Siggy were tired. Morning had come, but between the time difference and the fighting they'd lost a night's sleep. Earlier, Mama had doctored Alf's head. He'd have a scar, but hidden in his hair. Then they'd gone with a few others to look for the arrows fired during the night. They found the cockroach Alf had killed. It was half eaten. The guard too. Jhek tried to remove the guard's sunglasses, but they were attached to the side of his head. He lifted the guard's hair and saw that the stems grew into the skin above the ear. He pulled hard and they ripped out. He stepped back in shock. The bulbous, compound eyes glistened darkly with iridescent hues.

"We've always wondered what the guards really looked like," said Farlin. "They seem human, but never completely."

"They're half-human," said Mia coldly, "and half-human is no human."

Siggy examined the sunglasses. They were like altered insect wings, with veins running through the lens and forming the rims. He put them to his eyes. At first he saw nothing, just darkness, then he saw the world in pale, blue-violet hues, faint and delicate.

They returned to the tilting and Farlin and Jhek began to learn how to shoot a bow and arrow. They'd heard legends that such weapons existed before the Golden Ones came and outlawed them. Alf and Siggy watched them struggling to hit a tree trunk.

"They're a bit old to be learning about weapons," said Siggy.

"There's no choice," said Alf.

Mia came over to watch Jhek and Farlin shooting. After a while she tried it too. Three times in a row she hit her target.

"You're the one to use the bow," said Jhek. "We must be getting too old. I couldn't hit the side of a tilting if I tried."

But they did keep trying and slowly got better. Farlin asked Mia and the boys to teach others while he went to the forest to find ways to make their own bows and arrows.

"Take a machete," said Alf. "You might need it."

Hardly had he left when a group of men and women came out of the forest and stopped at the gate of the tilting. With them were a few boys.

"Who's in charge here?" asked one of the men.

"Our elector deserted," said Mia. "What do you want?"

"My name's Vanvir," said the man. "Most of us are electors from our tiltings. We came to find out what's been happening. I'm from the Lancet tilting on the other side of Golden Hill. We were attacked last night. Only three of us survived. All the girls were taken."

"Our tilting was also attacked," said another man. "Late in the night. Five of us made it, but the girls are gone too."

"But our tilting wasn't attacked," said a woman. "We've kept strictly to the law."

"We kept to the law too, but we were attacked," said Vanvir. "The Golden Ones are angry."

"Whether you fight or not you might be attacked," said Jhek. "Nova has fought and so far we have survived, or at least most of us. If we work together we might be able to defeat them."

"You can't defeat the Golden Ones," said the woman. "They're special—holy."

"They're trash," said Mia fiercely. "I know. I've been behind the Golden Doors. They took the girls for breeding. They know their stock might soon need replenishing."

The woman was shocked.

"What do you mean you've been behind the Golden Doors?" she asked. "The elevated never return. They spend their lives above us all, with no wants or worries."

"Haven't you heard about her?" said Vanvir. "She's the one who escaped."

"I heard, but didn't believe it," said the woman. "Why would anyone want to escape the pyramid?"

"Because they're evil," said Mia. "How do you think the guards are bred? Haven't you noticed that they're always men? Why else would young women be 'elevated'? They're bred, discarded and eaten."

The woman began to shake. "My daughter was taken last year," she said. "She was only fourteen. I thought … I thought she was being looked after. That's what the guards said."

Someone put their arms around her and held her tight as she began to wail in grief.

After this there were no more questions. Everyone in the group wanted to fight. They were taken around and shown how to set out their defenses and make simple weapons. They were given a laser or flashlight and a lighter to start a fire, which was all Alf and Siggy could offer. Those who still had a tilting hurried home. The rest stayed and joined Nova.

39 – Survivor

Evening came. Flocks of vivid birds flew round and round the tilting crying rhythmically. There were far more than normal but they refused to settle on the building. A cloud of black and brown seabirds flapped slowly past, headed towards the ocean. Not a single oaplah rose into sight above the forest canopy as the sun weakened.

A massive pile of wood stood in the courtyard, ready to be lit. Extra firewood stood in piles. Alf and Siggy had caught an hour of troubled sleep but were tired. There was little to eat. A few roots had been dug and cooked. Some were edible, barely; others not.

The gates were closed and the bolts pushed to. Many long sticks had been sharpened to defend against the cockroaches and guards. Primitive shields had also been made from woven vines to protect from metal slugs. As for stopping the underground creatures, so little was known about them that nothing could be done. Alf and Siggy were the only ones to have survived an attack.

Just before the sun disappeared Siggy lit the bonfire. All around the tilting people stood ready to fight. They had enough light and batteries to last the night, but Alf was worried. The flashlights were buying time, but only a day or two. They wouldn't last forever—neither would the firewood, or the food. Sooner or later they'd become scarce and their defenses would weaken.

The night was tense but the battle, if it could be called that, was low key. The lasers kept the few flying cockroaches that appeared at bay, and a number of guards were spotted out in the forest. At midnight the lookout from the top of the tilting shouted that a neighboring building, one that had chosen to fight, was being attacked. Siggy and Alf ran up the stairs to look. The tilting was lit up from the glow of their bonfire, but it was too far away to see clearly and the defense wall was obscured by the trees. There was nothing to do but watch and wait. Suddenly the neighbor's fire dimmed and shouts were heard. Within minutes darkness took over in that sector. The wind shifted and the smell of burning flesh hung in the air for the rest of the night.

***

The next morning Farlin, Jhek and two other men went to find out what happened at the neighboring tilting. They came back carrying a man on a makeshift litter. A chunk of his calf was missing, bitten off cleanly. He was feverish.

"He's the only survivor," said Jhek. "A pile of wood fell on him and he was hidden underneath."

"What happened?" asked Mama, wiping the man's brow with a damp cloth.

"We're not sure," said Farlin. "The wall was down in one place—undermined. Strangest of all was the bonfire. It was piled high with guards."

"Why would they do that?" said Alf. "Better to fight than cremate bodies."

The survivor groaned. His face was flushed.

"He's burning up," said Mama. "His wound must be poisoning him."

The man struggled to sit up. He looked around him desperately.

"Hush, hush," said Mia, bending down beside him. "You're with friends."

Her voice calmed the man and he lay back down. His gaze cleared, though his breathing was heavy.

"What happened?" asked Mia.

"They came," he said. "The ground, under the wall, it heaved and the wall fell. A cockroach landed on top of the tilting. It was huge, far bigger than the others. It vomited, choking us with bile. The cockroach spoke … it had strange speech … like nothing we'd ever heard. Then the guards rushed in."

The man arched his back and closed his eyes. Finally he relaxed. He was silent for a long time.

"And then what?" asked Mia. "We have to know."

He opened his eyes, his gaze glazed and distant.

"And then what?" insisted Mia, gently shaking his shoulder.

"The guards … the guards flung themselves onto the fire. It was strange. They wailed and cried out, but stayed, burning. They smothered the flames. Then the others came."

Mama put her hand on Mia.

"No more," she said. "He's going."

A moment later the man let out a long sigh. They waited, but there was no in-breath.

40 – Counter Tactics

The leaders were in Mia's room. It was early afternoon and the quietest place to have a meeting. They'd buried the man in the forest beside the others who had died.

"We need to change our defenses," said Siggy.

"How?" said Jhek. "We've done all we can."

"We heard what happened at that tilting last night," said Siggy. "The roaches used a different strategy, and it worked."

"I agree," said Mia. "Got any ideas, O bright one?"

Siggy smiled. "One or two," he said. "How hard is it to get the juice from the tilting tree?"

"Easy," said Mia. "Make a cut beneath a branch and hang a bucket under it. It drips out quickly. You don't need much to build with, just enough to soften the clay."

"Great," said Siggy, jumping up. "I need to get to work," and he ran down the stairs.

"Siggy, come back," cried Alf. "We're not finished," but he didn't stop.

"He's an odd one," said Jhek.

"But clever," said Farlin. "In the meantime we need more weapons, and light."

"I agree," said Jhek. "Alf and Siggy have to go back and get more."

"It's not that easy," said Alf. "In our world we are considered children. We are limited in what we can do."

"But you got stuff before," said Mia.

"Only because an adult took us to stores and exchanged a golden slug for money beforehand."

"We have lots of slugs now," said Farlin. "Is gold valuable there too?"

"Yes, very, except you can buy much more than you can here."

"Gold is useless here now," said Jhek, "except to throw at people."

"If the roaches win," said Farlin, "they'll get it all back in exchange for food. They know that. In the meantime, Alf has to return and get what he can. And he has to do it quickly. We might not last another night."

"Then an adult has to come with us," said Alf, "to help carry stuff if nothing else."

The two men looked uneasy. The idea of going to another world was strange to them. Instar was the only place they knew.

"I'll go," said Mia, sensing their unease.

"No," said Farlin. "I will. We need strength and size to bring weapons back, nothing less will do." He stood up. "If we must go, sooner is better."

They descended the stairs and saw that Siggy had already organized one group to get tilting juice, and another to dig clay.

"We're going back," Alf said to him.

"Not me," said Siggy. "I have to stay. Take someone bigger, they'd be more useful."

"We already decided that," said Alf.

"Good," said Siggy, running off to join the collecting group.

Mia helped Alf and Farlin fill the two packs with golden slugs. They'd been collected into piles, ready to be thrown.

"I want to go too," said Mia as they put on their packs.

"No," said Farlin. "You stay. The more here the better."

Mia hung her head, then she threw her arms around Alf and gave him a quick kiss.

* * *

Alf dropped into the passageway. Farlin came a moment later. He looked at the walls in wonder and touched them. Their silvery hue reflected his gesture. Alf led the way towards the door. There were fresh scratches. Deep ones. Alf turned the handle. It spun in his hand but the door didn't open.

"Drat," said Alf. "It's not opening."

Farlin looked at him. "What does that mean?"

"Sometimes it opens and sometimes not," said Alf. "There's no way of telling."

"So what now?"

"We wait," said Alf. "There's nothing else to do—unless you want to go back."

The Darkling Beasts

"No," said Farlin. "If we don't get help from your world then we are doomed. Better to stay."

They sat down and waited, and it wasn't long before Alf was sound asleep with his head against Farlin's shoulder. So it was that he didn't notice that Farlin also fell asleep from exhaustion.

41 – Alf's World

Alf and Farlin woke when the roaring started in the forest. They felt the ground tremble around them. It was dark. Pitch black.

"You awake?" asked Farlin.

"Yes," whispered Alf. "We've slept too long.

"Try the door," said Farlin. "We must get out of here."

Alf stood up and fumbled for the door handle. He found it and pulled. The door opened. The Hall lights were lit and the sound of voices filled the air. Alf knew instantly that the carnival was on. For a few moments Alf and Farlin were blinded and had to cover their eyes.

"Let's go," said Alf when their eyes had adjusted. "I hope we're not too late."

They stepped into the Hall.

"What's this?" said Farlin, looking around him half in fear, half in amazement.

"It's a Hall of Mirrors," said Alf. Then he remembered that the Instars didn't have mirrors. "They're made to reflect your image, like still water on a pond."

Farlin touched the glass as if it was going to be water. He was surprised by how hard the surface was.

Alf smiled. "This way," he said, leading him down the passage. "Be careful with your backpack, glass can shatter if you hit it with something hard."

They made their way through the Hall, their images reaching into the infinite. Twice Farlin walked into a corner.

"What kind of world is this?" said Farlin. "This is too strange!"

Alf laughed. "It's not all like this. In fact, a Hall of Mirrors is rare these days. It's built for fun and is completely old fashioned and out of date. This space is just where the portal is."

They came to the exit door and stepped into the night. The carnival was in full swing. They were still in the field outside Wendover. Farlin's jaw dropped. The merry-go-round went round and round, its horses rising and falling to music; lights flashed on the Ferris wheel as it turned; speakers blared from all directions and a group of teenagers were shouting and tossing balls at gophers. Alf looked at Farlin and decided not to explain. Whatever he said would not make much sense. He spotted Cam sitting at the ticket table. His back was to them.

"Cam," he called. "Cam!"

Cam turned.

"What the fish flakes," he exclaimed, jumping up. "You're back! Where'd you go?"

"Where do you think? You should have stayed with us."

Cam charged into the Hall and rushed down the passageways. Alf dropped his pack and met him at the portal. The door said, 'DON'T'. Cam touched it.

"This has never been here," he said. "Where'd it come from?" He went to turn the handle.

"Don't," said Alf. "It's a dangerous time."

Cam let go of the handle.

"Trust me," said Alf. "Now is not the time. And besides, we need your help, quickly."

"Where's Siggy," asked Cam.

"Fighting," said Alf. "There's a battle going on."

Cam nodded and touched Alf's head where he'd been hit.

Alf winced. "I'm fine," he said.

They went back to Farlin and Alf introduced them.

Cam looked Farlin up and down. Farlin's clothes were strange: roughly woven, hand sewn and simply cut.

"You're one of those back-to-the-land hippies," said Cam at last, finding a label, and he put out his hand. "Meaning no offense, of course. I'm like that myself."

Farlin took Cam's hand uncertainly, but was too polite to comment

The Darkling Beasts

on Cam's appearance. He was shocked to see a pregnant man in a greasy baseball cap and a one-size-too-small t-shirt.

"Lock the door and close the Hall," said Alf. "We have work to do."

"I know we got a bunch of dough from that golden ball," said Cam, "but it won't last forever. I gotta earn a living."

Alf bent over and opened the top of his pack. A pile of gold glistened inside. Cam's eye's opened.

"No problem," he said, pulling out his keys and locking the door. He put away the cash table and turned off the Hall lights. "Let's go to Ester's and talk."

They made their way down the aisles, weaving in and out between the crowd. Farlin stared, all eyes and ears. There were stalls hung to the rafters with stuffed animals of all colors, balloon men selling, barkers barking, games of toss and throw and bowl, and candy floss women touting their wares.

"Come to me! Come to me, me lovelies!" shouted a bearded woman as they passed her trailer. "Peek in here for more sights than you'll ever see in a month of Sundays!"

"Over 'ere! Over 'ere!" called the Spinning Man. "Come see me spin!"

The fireworks crew set off a round of rockets. They screamed into the air and burst with a series of thunderclaps and great showers of colored sparks. Farlin threw himself onto the ground and cowered. Cam looked at him in amazement.

"It's okay," said Alf, running over. "It's part of the show," and he helped him up.

As he brushed off his clothes Farlin looked at the crowd and saw that they were not in the least disturbed by such a great display of power and strength.

Ester had set up her stall at the edge of the carnival. The table for the workers sat out of the crowd behind her. "Alf," she cried when she saw him, giving him a hug. "Where's Siggy?"

Then she saw Farlin. She froze and stared.

"You're from Instar," she said, her voice hardly audible.

Farlin nodded. "We've come for supplies. The Golden Ones have been uncovered. Battles rage."

"Well, that's fine and dandy," said Cam, "but business first. Let's eat," and he marched over to the table and sat down.

Ester brought stew and freshly baked bread slathered with butter. She stayed and cleaned Alf's wound as they talked. She could hardly take her eyes off Farlin. Alf pulled a few slugs from his pack and put them on the table.

"Cam, we need weapons, lights, tools," said Alf, "anything we can carry."

Cam reached out and took a golden ball. His hands shook.

"How many did you bring over?" he asked.

"These two packs," said Farlin. "As much as they could hold without breaking."

"That's a lot of loot to fence," said Cam. "I mean, that's a lot of gold to cash in. I don't know anyone who would have that much cash on hand."

"It doesn't matter," said Alf. "There's tons where this came from. We can barter."

"But no one will believe us if we say it's gold. No one walks around with lumps like this. It's not done."

"What about your pawnbroker, Andy?" asked Alf.

Cam looked doubtful. "It's a start," he said. "But you saw how he had to dig into every nook and cranny to give us a tenth the worth of that last slug. I looked up the price of gold and he really shafted us. Still, we can try in the morning. And if he doesn't have it, perhaps he knows someone who will."

"We don't have time," said Farlin. "My people are fighting and dying right now."

"You're deadly serious?" said Cam. "This is for real?"

"Completely," said Farlin. There was no mistaking his tone.

"I'll give you all the money I have," said Ester. "I can get some from the bank machine tomorrow, but most of it will have to wait until Monday."

Alf groaned. "It's Saturday night. I forgot. Most shops will be closed tomorrow."

"What are you talking about?" said Farlin. "Just get what we need and go."

"It doesn't work like that here," said Ester. "Only some days are working days. I have to get back to work now, but the carnival will be over

117

The Darkling Beasts

in an hour. We close at one o'clock. Cam, you go to the pawnbrokers and see what he can do. Let's meet again and hear the full story. Then Alf and Farlin can tell us exactly what they need."

Cam got up to leave.

"And tell your mum to come too," said Ester. "I'm sure she will have something to say."

* * *

Alf and Farlin sat at Ester's table. They were so hungry they ate seconds, then thirds. Alf had cinnamon buns and soda for desert. Farlin looked around at everything that was happening, but his eyes kept wandering to Ester as she served her customers.

"How long has she been here?" he asked Alf.

"About twenty years; at least that's what I've been told. She came through the Hall of Mirrors too. Cam's uncle found her. She was only a young teen, about Mia's age."

"And then what?" asked Farlin.

"I don't know much," said Alf. "You'll have to ask her. She lived with Cam's uncle until he died. He left Cam the Hall and her some money. She bought this food vending business and has been doing it ever since."

Farlin nodded and continued to examine her carefully. Every now and then she would turn and look at Farlin and their eyes would meet.

The crowds began to thin; people were tired and going home. At one o'clock sharp a large rocket soared into the air and exploded with a massive bang that echoed off the surrounding hills. Green and red streamers blossomed outwards, whistling as they fell. This was followed by sparkles crackling in the air. Lastly came dozens of small explosions. Farlin looked up in awe. He'd never dreamed of such a thing.

"Are they safe," he asked.

"Only at a distance," said Alf. "If you're not careful they'll cause all sorts of damage."

"What kind of damage?" asked Farlin, suddenly sitting up.

"Lots," said Alf, getting his drift. "Huge lots."

42 - Siblings

Farlin helped Ester put things into her truck while Alf washed dishes. "I've never seen so much iron in all my life," said Farlin. "They use iron for everything here. Instar only has enough for essential tools. Where does it all come from?"

"From mines," said Ester, "but I don't know the details."

"It's everywhere," said Farlin, gesturing. "Look at all these pots and pans and knives and forks. And your big box there, with iron wheels, what's that?"

"That's a truck," said Ester. "And you're right; I never really thought about how much we use iron. There's tons and tons of it here."

Suddenly the truck next to Ester's started up its engine. Farlin dropped the box he was carrying and staggered backwards.

"What's happening?" he gasped.

Alf laughed. "Sorry," he said. "The look on your face was so funny. These 'boxes' have engines inside and can move about on their wheels. The big ones are called trucks, and the small ones, cars."

Farlin stared as the truck slowly pulled away. Ester ran to the driver and gave him a sandwich and waved as he drove off.

"I'm not sure I'd ever get used to this place," said Farlin, picking up the box.

By one-thirty the carnival had shut down. Most people were staying the night and heading out in the morning. Those who weren't were already driving out of the field and down the road. Farlin kept staring at all this activity. He asked questions about everything, but especially about the floodlights. He was disappointed that they weren't easily portable. Finally Cam came back with his mum. Farlin's eyes opened when he saw her size. All the folk in Instar were slim.

"Alf—you eel," she shouted, and he vanished into here ample bosom. "What happened to your head?" She gave the wound a cursory glance and whacked him across the ear. "You'll be fine in no time. It's just a scratch. Cam says that Siggy is fighting too. He shouldn't be fighting. He'll just get into trouble. Oh, he's a rascal."

"But he's fighting horrible insects and their offspring," said Alf.

"Insects," shouted Cam's mum. "Fighting insects? Then he's a bigger fool than I thought. What kind of insects?"

"Cockroaches," said Farlin. "They're huge, deadly and murderous. They usurped the Golden Ones. Siggy does right to fight them."

Cam's mum gave Farlin a critical look up and down. She liked what she saw.

"Well, he's still a fool," said Cam's mum. "If he wants to get rid of cockroaches he should use a good dose of Lively's Guaranteed Cockroach Cruncher. I used it once and that was the end of that lot, I'll tell ya. Never bothered me again. Now, what's this meeting about? I'm tired. Give me a seat."

Alf ran and got her a chair to sit on. It squeaked loudly as her weight descended. Everyone stared, hoping the chair wouldn't collapse. It didn't.

"What's that stuff you were talking about?" asked Farlin. "Does it really kill cockroaches?"

"Sure does," said Cam's mum. "Deader than a dormouse run over by all eighteen wheels of a big rig."

Farlin wasn't sure what a dormouse or an eighteen wheel big rig was, but the rest sounded good.

"Where do you get this killer stuff?" he asked.

"Got tons of it at home," said Cam's mum. "Like I said, it's called Lively's Guaranteed Cockroach Cruncher. Cam uses it. Any decent hardware store should have it—if it's right decent, that is. Not all are. Not by a long shot. I once—"

"So, Cam, what did you find out from the pawnbrokers?" injected Ester, hoping to head his mum off before she got going.

"Nothing much," said Cam. "Two hundred bully-boys is all he had—and he still wanted me to leave a gold slug as surety. Doubt I'll ever see the rest."

"Tell us the whole tale," said Ester. "Then we'll know best how to help."

Alf and Farlin recounted all that had happened from the time Mia had been elevated. Cam's mum sat listening as if it were a fairy tale gone bad, but the two bags of gold had her thinking twice.

"It all sounds a bit far fetched," said Cam's mum. "Why would anyone let a swarm of disgusting roaches run the world?"

"And how's that different to what we have here?" asked Cam.

Cam's mum opened her mouth to answer, but snapped it shut again. "Still," she said after a moment, "I'd just poison the buggers."

"It's not farfetched," said Ester quietly. "That's how I came here. I ran away instead of being elevated, as they call it. Luckily I found the doorway under the hollow tree."

"What was the name of your tilting?" asked Farlin.

"Riveron," said Ester. "The one by Taskent creek."

"Then you are my sister," said Farlin, stepping towards her and holding out his hands. "My parents always talked about how you vanished rather than be elevated. I was born a year later. Your name is Finnue, Finnue of Riveron."

"I knew ... I knew," said Ester, taking his hands. "You looked so familiar, and yet I'd never seen you."

She threw her arms around Farlin and held him tight, tears streaming from her eyes.

"Looks like this story is for real," said Cam. "Gold nuggets by the dozen, brothers meeting sisters, Alf disappearing an' all. So what do we need?"

"Two things, for sure," said Alf, "cockroach killer and fireworks—the biggest bangers and rockets we can get. And guns, if we can."

"Guns are hard to come by," said Cam. "Leastwise, hard to get quickly. All I have is my shotgun, but it's at home."

"What about fireworks?" asked Alf. "The fireworks crew is still here."

"Aye," said Cam. "The Campbells are worth a try. I'll go now before it gets too late. Give me more of those gold slugs and I'll see what I can do. Meanwhile, get some rest. We drive out of here in a few hours."

43 – Battle at Nova

Siggy spent the rest of the day directing the construction of new defenses. They used clay mixed with tilting juice to fill in the windows of the common room and the first five stories above it. Narrow slits and small round holes were left to repel attackers. Holes were cut in the floors

The Darkling Beasts

and crude ladders allowed access from floor to floor. All doors were filled in except for the common room. It was narrowed so that only one person could squeeze through with difficulty and the doorway shaped to receive premade bricks.

Siggy marveled at how quickly the tilting tree juice allowed for construction. When the clay dried it was tough, strong, flexible, and impervious to water. When the juice was applied full strength to a wall or floor, however, it soaked in and made the clay soft again. The only problem was its drying time. It hardened the clay quickly but not quickly enough. When they were done they lit fires or laid embers beside the fresh mud in each room. By sunout the rooms smelled of smoke but were secure.

The top room was also defended. They filled in the windows and drilled holes in the ceiling, big enough for a spear to fit through. Then four men with supplies sealed themselves inside.

Sunout came. Siggy had arranged a series of smaller bonfires all around the building and one was lit. Lasers and flashlights were shone into the forest as darkness shut in the world. Siggy was the last into the common room and they slid premade bricks into the reshaped doorway. They were heavy and solid and could only be removed from inside. Then they waited.

Nothing happened. People lay on the floor in exhaustion or fell asleep. Guards were set in pairs and changed every hour. The forest was quiet.

"It's too quiet," said Siggy.

He was lying on a blanket on the fifth floor. Mia sat next to him.

"It is," she said. "But it's also nice. Listen to the wind sigh in the trees."

Siggy listened. The trees were sighing. A sea breeze was blowing inland. It rose and fell in waves.

"If you listen hard, you can hear the wind-waves coming from far away," said Mia after a while, putting her hand lightly on Siggy's back.

He didn't answer. He had fallen asleep.

***

At midnight the howling in the forest around them suddenly began. Siggy and Mia awoke bathed in sweat, their hearts pounding.

"Great beasts are out there," cried a watchman. "The ground is heaving towards the gates."

Siggy looked down. The fire he'd lit was almost out. He rushed to the common room. Here the watch had fallen asleep in exhaustion.

"The fires! The fires!" shouted Siggy.

He grabbed a bow, lit an arrow fitted with dried grass soaked in oil, and shot it out a window slit. It hit the mark and the bonfire flared up. He ran to the opposite side. The guard had another arrow ready but was fumbling to light it. Siggy snapped his lighter and it flared up. He shot, and another bonfire burned.

Flashlights were shining out the window slits. Many were focused to the right of the gate. There the earth was heaving. Something was underneath and burrowing towards the wall.

"What kind of monster is that?" asked Jhek of no one in particular.

Siggy handed his bow to Jhek. "When it comes, shoot. You have more strength than me."

"But not as good an aim," said Jhek. "Still, you are right. I will try."

Siggy went up a couple of flights and found Mia looking out a window. She had a flashlight.

"There are guards in the forest," she said. "Lots of them."

Without warning the ground under the wall beside the gate heaved upwards. The wall cracked and fell and one gatepost toppled inwards, twisting the metal gate. For a moment dark shapes were visible, like the back of a giant beast.

"There's more than one," shouted Mia. "They're working together."

An arrow flew down from the tower and sunk in deep. There was a roar, a howl unlike any creature of the earth. Then the ground heaved and crumpled as the beast fled the tilting.

"Good shot," cried Siggy to Jhek out the window, but his voice was drowned out.

A great shout went up in the forest and guards poured in through the gaping hole in the wall. For a moment they stopped, surprised not to see anyone in the courtyard. A cry came from the sky. A voice called out: hollow, high-pitched, insistent, full of clicks and whistles, and yet with meaning. The guards shouted again and divided into two groups. Each one raced towards a bonfire and flung themselves onto it. They screamed and cried out in pain. They thrashed terribly as they sizzled and burned—but they stayed put, as if by an iron will.

The Darkling Beasts

"Quick," shouted Siggy to Jhek. "Light another woodpile," and in a moment a blazing arrow fell into a fresh pile of wood. It began to burn, but a guard flung himself on the small blaze and put it out.

Suddenly a great stench filled the air and drops of brown liquid fell from the heights. It was nauseating and people retched and vomited. More guards poured into the gates. They carried long spears and shields. They too stopped in surprise. Flashlights and lasers from the tilting played across their faces and forced them to hold up their shields. Then they charged. But there was only one stairway up the tilting. They were pushed off and pierced by those within as they tried to attack.

Another cry sounded from high in the air. In an instant cockroaches flew towards the tilting from the forest. Some, blinded by the flashlights, crashed into the building and fell to the ground. Others clung to the walls. They reached in through the openings with their barbed legs. A few inside, caught unawares, were slashed and cut, but there was no way for the roaches to get in. They were pierced through by spears, had their legs cut off with machetes or were pounded by stones.

Suddenly an ungodly hue and cry came from the top of the tower. It was so loud that the people inside quailed and groaned in fear—but so too did the guards.

"What was that?" shouted Siggy over the din. He was busy throwing slugs out the window slits at anything that moved outside.

"I don't know," said Mia, "but it sounded bad."

"They're leaving! They're leaving!" voices shouted.

The cockroaches were flying away, or scurrying back into the forest and trampling over guards in their haste. The guards ran here and there in disarray, trying to find an exit. In moments the courtyard was empty of all but the dead and badly wounded.

"Jhek, light two fires," shouted Siggy down the ladder holes.

Within moments two fresh piles of wood were burning.

Jhek climbed upstairs to the fifth floor. Siggy and Mia were moving from window slit to window slit trying to make out what was happening below.

"I think they're gone," said Jhek, looking out. "They retreated. Something happened upstairs."

"We must be able to communicate with the top room," said Siggy. "We'll have to fix that tomorrow."

They went through the rooms, checking how people were doing. Children were crying and women were hushing them. Others were setting out their weapons, ready for another attack. The stench from the burning bodies outside and the brown juice poured from above made the airless rooms suffocating and miserable.

"We need wind," said Siggy. "A fresh wind."

Hardly had he spoken when the wind outside picked up. It rustled and shook the trees and poured around the tilting. Fresh air blew through the narrow holes and slits and the stench eased.

"Well done, Siggy," said Mama, coming over and patting him on the back. "You're a wizard too, I see."

44 - Aftermath

Morning came. The wind dropped and the stench thickened. The bricks were removed from the common room door and Jhek, Mia and Siggy climbed to the topmost room with a bucket of tilting juice and a spade. Jhek boosted Siggy up to the roof, then he and Mia brushed the juice onto the filled-in doorway.

Siggy walked around the roof. The whole area stank and was stained deep brown. One spot, near a hole, was black. Suddenly a spear stabbed viciously out of one of the holes.

"Hey!" shouted Siggy. "It's us. It's morning. You're safe!"

A deep groan came from inside.

"Are you alright?" he shouted, but he only heard groaning. He didn't dare look into one of the holes. He climbed back down and Jhek continued to drive his spade into the softened wall, while Mia splashed the area with juice. Finally they broke through and made a small opening.

"Let us out," groaned a man.

They worked quickly and soon had the four men on the stairs. They were haggard and sick, but began to revive in the fresh air.

"What happened?" asked Mia when they were a little better.

"He came," said one of them. "The king. We heard him land. Then he started talking. I've never heard such a voice. Like wind in a narrow place and dry leaves underfoot."

"We heard it too," said Jhek. "He was giving orders to the guards and roaches."

"A terrible smell poured out of him," said the man. "Juice seeped in through the holes. It made us sick. We retched and heaved. Jonan there, he poked upwards with a spear. You got him, didn't you Jonan?"

"I did," said Jonan. "I heard a crunch as the point went in. But it didn't go in far enough, I think. He cried out and flew away. We've been suffocating in that hell-hole ever since. Next time you'll leave us with tilting juice to make more holes to breathe."

They helped the men to their feet and accompanied them to the courtyard where they were treated like heroes. Then they held a council.

"They won't attack the same way," said Siggy. "They're much too clever. Still, we'll have to defend the roof and the lower sections again as best as we can."

"What do you think they're going to do next?" asked Mia.

Siggy shook his head. "I'm not sure. I'm trying to imagine what I'd do if I were them."

"Perhaps the king roach is dead," said Mama.

"Perhaps," said Jhek. "But if they are like real insects they'll soon have a new one."

"I hope the roach king wasn't killed," said Mia. "I hope he's slowed down and cannot attack for a while."

"We cannot rely on that," said Mama.

"No, we can't," agreed Jhek, "but what more can we do?"

"First of all, some have to visit the nearby tiltings and find out what happened to them," said Siggy. "In the meanwhile, I have a few ideas."

The rest of the day was spent hauling the dead guards to the forest and renewing the defenses. They fashioned a long, hollow clay pipe leading from the top room to the bottom ones. This would allow communication. They hauled more wood to the bonfires and patched up the wall as best they could, though it was clear that this would only slow things down. Siggy had them dig a maze of pits and trenches all around the courtyard and in them they set sharpened spikes pointing upwards. The holes were covered with brush, plastered over with a thin layer of tilting clay, and then sprinkled with dirt and ashes to disguise them. In the end it was impossible to tell where they were and markers had to be set up and guards posted to warn those who were coming back with firewood.

In the afternoon the ones who had gone to the other tiltings began to return. Most had good news, or at least not bad news, but some didn't. Two tiltings had been attacked early in the night and only a couple survived to tell the tale. The defense wall had been toppled, the roach king landed on the roof, and the guards flung themselves onto the fires. Then, in the darkness, a terrible stench went up and the tilting was swamped with guards attacking from below, while flying cockroaches swarmed through every window and door. The other tiltings had been left alone, though some had caught glimpses of guards deep in the forest.

"It seems they tested their method before attacking us," said Jhek. "Luckily, we were one step ahead."

Siggy looked worried. "They'll try something unexpected," he said gloomily. "I feel it in my bones. Our only hope is for Alf and Farlin to get back here quickly. And we'll need much more than a few flashlights to make a difference."

45 – Siggy appears.

Farlin couldn't rest. He was exhausted beyond any tiredness he'd ever felt before, but the sights and sounds of this crazy world were whirling around in his head: crowds of people, music blasting, trucks with loud engines, bright lights in the middle of the night and fireworks exploding in the air above his head. He wondered how people could live like this? It was crazy. And he'd met his sister. His sister! Everyone in his family spoke of her as dead. Her 'death' had troubled his parents and cast a shadow over them.

Alf stirred beside Farlin. They were in the Hall of Mirrors, lying on blankets. Farlin turned over and tried his other side. The faint light filtering in through the skylights let him see his face in the mirrors. This disturbed him. He wasn't used to looking at himself. He pulled the blanket further over his head and closed his eyes. Somehow, he fell asleep.

"Wake up—wake up," said Cam loudly, shaking Farlin's shoulder.

Farlin groaned and sat up. Alf was already pulling on his shoes.

"They wouldn't sell me any fireworks," said Cam. "Bloody idiots. I offered them three gold nuggets, but they refused to part with any. They thought I was trying to con them with fool's gold. They're the fools if ever there were any."

Farlin brushed his hair out of his eyes. "Now what?" he asked.

"We've got to get out of here, and quick," said Cam. "It's late and we're the last ones left."

Farlin and Alf stepped out of the Hall and into the field. Cam's mum sat in her truck with Harry in the passenger seat. He didn't look happy. Ester was standing beside her van talking to another woman. Otherwise the field was empty, with worn down grass and litter everywhere. Farlin had realized that trucks and cars moved, but what he'd taken to be a whole city had vanished. Instead, another town sat on a hill beyond the field and rose up layer after layer to the top. There was no defense wall, no tiltings, but many houses lying close to each other in a semi-organized jumble. He looked up at the sky, and screamed. Everyone turned towards him and his sister came running.

"The sun! The sun!" he cried. "It's falling from the sky!"

"It's okay," said Ester, taking his arm. "The sun moves in this world. It crosses the whole sky during the day and is gone by night."

For a moment Farlin stared at her as if she was mad. Then he saw how everyone except Alf was looking at him strangely.

"It's true," said Alf. "It was just as strange for us to see your sun get smaller and vanish at night."

"Why didn't you tell me back at the tilting?" said Farlin.

"Would you have believed me?" said Alf.

Farlin shook his head. "No," he admitted, "I'd have thought you mad. I suppose you were wise to keep your mouth shut."

"We also have a moon and stars," said Alf. "We couldn't see them last night because it was cloudy."

Farlin didn't understand what Alf was talking about.

"You're going to ride with me in my van," said Ester, leading her brother away. "We have lots of talking to do."

***

They drove down the freeway in convoy, heading for Cam's mum's place. Alf was sitting with Cam and wondering how Farlin was doing with Ester. They had a lot of catching up to do. They left the hilly landscape and bypassed towns and cities, the traffic getting heavier and then falling off again. Lunchtime came and Cam pulled into a rest stop. Ester gave them sandwiches and drinks and they headed off again. A couple of hours later they left the freeway. They dropped off Harry in Upper Farnon, then wound through ever smaller byroads before turning into the gate at Cam's mum's place. Alf was surprised at how happy he was to see the trailer home and the yard full of junked cars and beaten up sheds. The chickens squawked and fled the vehicles as they bounced down the rutted driveway. Finally they stopped and went into the house.

"Welcome! Welcome all!" boomed Cam's mum at the top of her lungs. "Come on in and make yourselves at home. Put up your feet, never mind the furniture. I'll make a pot of coffee."

Farlin sat on the living room sofa with Ester. He looked unsure of everything around him. Alf steered clear of Cam's lounger and sat on a chair he'd nabbed from the kitchen. Finally Cam came in and flopped into his favorite chair with a sigh.

"There's nothing like being at home," he said, putting his smelly feet on the rickety coffee table.

"What are we going to do about Siggy?" said Cam's mum, when she'd served the coffee. "Sounds like we have to get moving, and yet we've hardly done anything."

"We must get going," said Farlin. "I can't wait any longer. My tilting might be destroyed."

"There's no point in going back without something to fight with," said Alf.

"There's my shotgun," said Cam. "I only have one box of shells, though. We can get some tomorrow."

"We can't wait till tomorrow," said Farlin fiercely.

"There's no use fretting," said Cam's mum, laying her plump hand on Farlin's shoulder and massaging him a bit too long. "We need a plan. A plan. We gotta think."

The Darkling Beasts

"What we need are lights, guns and fireworks," said Alf, "though dynamite might be a better option."

"Dynamite," said Cam, suddenly sitting up. "Now that I might be able to get. If I had a permit."

"There's no time for permits," said Ester. "You have to get what you can and get going."

Cam considered for a moment. "There's Jimmy Tan. He's a road builder and excavator for the local council. He has dynamite for blasting rocks. Only problem is, I don't like the rat. He'll not give me any just out of spite. Besides, he has to account to the authorities for every stick he owns."

"And why didn't the Campbells sell you fireworks?" asked Ester.

"They're idiots and refused. Thought I was drunk, or mad," said Cam. "They didn't want my gold."

"It's so silly," said Ester. "Here we are, sitting on a fortune and no way to buy things because we don't have cash."

"Then we have to take it," said Farlin. "Where do the Campbells live, and Jimmy Tan?"

"The Campbells are an hour's drive away, and Jimmy is local," said Cam, "but we can't just go there and take it."

"And we can't just let people die because they won't sell us what we need," said Alf.

Cam's mum sat listening to the talk going back and forth. She heaved herself out of the sofa, opened the kitchen door and scooped up a cat. It was Kitty-o.

"Kitty-o," cried Alf, jumping up to pet her. "How did you get here?"

"Someone must have left the Hall door open," said Cam's mum.

"Not me," said Cam. "Never touched it."

"Nor me," said Ester.

"Me neither," said Alf.

"It was me," said Siggy, poking his head in the kitchen door.

46 – Felling

Siggy was gone. They'd tried to persuade him to stay but he said he wasn't much use once the fighting started. He'd headed up the hill towards the hollow tree and said he'd be back as quickly as possible. That was before nightfall. Now it was dark. Two bonfires were lit in the courtyard, everyone was inside and the doors sealed off. Upstairs, four men again manned the highest room, this time with tilting juice on the inside. They'd also stocked up with metal slugs and spiked balls shaped from clay soaked in tilting juice and baked in a fire. They were Siggy's idea and looked quite vicious.

"I don't like this waiting," said Mia. She was in the highest room in the lower section. Firelight flicked through the small openings left in the filled-in windows. Now and then she shone her laser into the forest but saw nothing. The forest was silent, too silent. Only in the distance had the howling begun.

Jhek was in the room with her. Mama was in the middle section helping to calm the children. Some were panicking, afraid of what was to come. Others wept silently. The night battles were too much for them. One child began to wail. It was a friend of Mia's and she went down the ladder to her. She held her tight and tried to calm her fears. At last she settled and Mia returned upstairs.

They waited. The hours passed and midnight came. Far in the distance they heard shouting and screams. It was so faint it was hard to make out and they had to strain to hear.

"Can you see what's happening?" Jhek asked, speaking into the tube they'd built to the upper room.

"Not really," came a voice back after a minute. "There was a fire at the Clairuz tilting and then it went out, but that was a while ago. We can't tell if the shouting is coming from there."

"I'd prefer to be back in my room," said Mia. "At least I'd have a chance to see what's going on."

"It fell!" shouted a voice from upstairs. "A great flame went up as it fell!"

A moment later a distant, crackling roar swept over the Nova tilting. The sound was rare, but known. When a tilting fell in a storm it sent up a roar as the trees shattered and the walls exploded. Mia heard people praying to the gods in the silence that followed. Survivors were rare from a fallen tilting, and unheard of if it happened at night.

Mia looked at Jhek. "They'll be here in less than an hour," she said.

They waited for half an hour. Then they lit all but two of the bonfires. Ten minutes later they were blazing brightly.

"They're here," said Jhek. "Look at them, the trees are alive with roaches."

Mia looked out and shone her laser. The forest was swarming with half-glimpsed life; the guards and roaches slinked within the trees or hid behind shields in order to keep away from the firelight and lasers. She saw one figure clearly as he darted from one tree to the next.

"They're carrying something," said Mia. "It looks like buckets."

"The ground, the ground is heaving," shouted a voice from upstairs. "They're coming from opposite sides."

The defense wall heaved and cracked in two places. Jhek and another man sent down arrows as quickly as they could, but the damaged gate and the wall on the other side of the tilting fell with a crash. A voice called out from the air. The cockroach king was circling the tower and commanding his brood. The first wave of guards rushed in and spread out. They were carrying buckets filled with liquid. They split into two groups that ran towards the fires, but were swallowed up in the pits as the ground gave way beneath them. The next wave backed away, shielding themselves from the rain of slugs, spiked balls and arrows that fell upon them.

An angry screech went up from the cockroach king. He began to chant the same phrase over and over again insistently. The guards mustered into two groups again, then, with a shout, they ran heedlessly towards the fires. The first ones again fell into the pits, but those that followed clambered and crawled over the dead and broken bodies as the pits filled up. They flung themselves mindlessly into the fires. The reek of burning flesh rose up. More and more piled in and soon the fires began to wane. Then the cockroaches attacked. They crawled over the tilting until it seethed as if alive. From inside the defenders jabbed with their sharpened sticks. They killed dozens, but they just kept coming. The roaches oozed rank juice over the walls and spat it through the holes. The defenders retched and vomited at the smell. If the spit touched human skin it burned fiercely; when it touched the eyes all sight was lost.

"Cover your hands and faces," cried Jhek. "Keep your body away from the holes; thrust with your spears," but there were more holes than spears and soon the screams of pain were overwhelming.

Young roaches started to enter the window slits. They were only two feet long but bit fiercely. The wounds burned and swelled rapidly.

"Stuff the holes! Stuff the holes," cried Mia, and people ran to fill the holes with jackets or shirts, but soon the fabric was torn away.

The air became unbreathable. There was no oxygen. Some began to be lightheaded and faint. Round and round the tower the cockroach king flew with his terrible, insistent voice, egging the attackers on.

"The guards are doing something to the tilting wall," came a voice from upstairs. "We can't see what it is. They've brought in huge shields and set them up around the seaward side. They're working underneath."

Then Mia smelled it: a sweet, milky smell, with a hint of peppermint. Tilting juice, lots of it.

"What are they doing?" said Jhek half to himself as he crushed a roach with his heel. He'd wrapped his face and hands in cloth and was jabbing at the holes. Every time he brought the spear inside it dripped more juice over the floor. By now the floor was slippery.

Suddenly Mia knew. They were softening the wall. They had to be. That's how they brought the Clairuz tilting down.

"All fighters downstairs," she screamed. "They're dissolving the wall. We must stop them or they'll fell the tilting."

It took a moment for her words to sink in. Then there was a mad rush for the ladder.

Downstairs in the common room they found the fighters staring at the wall and doing nothing. The clink and scrape of shovels and picks were clearly heard.

"What's happening?" shouted the Jhek. "Why are you just standing there?"

"Look at the holes," said one of the men. "At first we thrust our spears through the attack holes, but the guards either grabbed them and held them in place or blocked the hole with wooden plugs. Either way, the holes are useless. We can neither attack nor defend."

At that moment a piece of the seaward wall fell inwards and the tilting shuddered; a deep, structural shudder that could only spell doom. Jhek rushed forward and jammed his spear through the hole. A guard screamed, but another grabbed the shaft and held on. Jhek tried to pull it free but eventually it broke.

"We have to go outside and fight," said Mia.

"We can't," said Jhek. "We'd be as good as dead."

"We're as good as dead if we don't fight," said Mia. "I'd prefer to die fighting than stand here and wait to be slaughtered."

She went to the doorway and tried to lift one of the blocking bricks out of its groove but it was too heavy for her. Jhek came over and lifted it with her. The tilting groaned again and the seaward wall of the common room cracked and flaked. A large chunk fell outward. Suddenly many hands were shifting the heavy bricks.

"They're coming out," cried one of the guards from outside. "They're opening the door," and they thrust metal tipped spears through the doorway.

"Stand back," shouted a guard with authority. "Let the rats come out. We know what to do with them—and keep the girls alive for the king."

As they unblocked the doorway Mia could see outside. The guards formed a half circle around the entrance. Siggy had designed the altered door cleverly, but for defense. Only one at a time could climb inside over the half wall, but the same was true for going out. One by one they'd be picked off as they exited. The sweet smell of the tilting juice hung in the air and mixed with the awful odor of the cockroaches as the picks and shovels worked away at the seaward wall. Through the doorway the insistent voice of the cockroach king sounded louder and louder and the tilting groaned again. The children upstairs screamed. The tilting couldn't last much longer.

A whistle sounded, as if rising into the air. It was followed by a blinding flash that lit the night and threw the guards into stark relief. Then came a thundering boom—and another and another. A whooshing sound was followed by an orange-hued light which stayed hanging high in the air. It flickered constantly but kept burning. The guards fled. A thousand dry wings sounded as the cockroaches flew away. The cockroach king called out. He hissed and rasped. Two loud reports followed one after the other and the king was silent.

"It's Siggy and Alf," cried Mia. "It has to be!" She ran to the door. The courtyard was quickly emptying. High in the sky hung the orange light, gently floating earthwards. Beyond the gate a pregnant man stood with a long metal stick. Beside him were Farlin and Alf. A woman was there too, and Siggy. They threw sticks at the guards which exploded at their heels with a shattering bang, louder than anything Mia had ever heard before. More streaks of light shot upwards and exploded with many cascading colors in the air. It was terrifying yet beautiful.

"It's them, they've come," cried Mia, turning and shouting into the tilting. "It's Alf and Farlin and Siggy. Get out, get out before the tilting falls—tell the people in the top room."

There was a mad scramble as the spell was broken and everyone awoke to the danger. Within minutes they'd widened the door and a steady stream of people was exiting. Others were scrambling out the hole the guards had made.

Jhek ran over to the group outside the gate. "Get away from here," he shouted. "The tilting is going to fall."

Everyone gathered to the landward side of the defense wall and looked up. The orange light overhead began to gutter.

"Shoot another," Alf called to Cam.

Cam fitted a flare into the gun and raised his arm. The flare whooshed high into the night sky and began its slow decent on its parachute.

They watched as a hole appeared in the door of the topmost room. It seemed to take a long time.

"Hurry! Hurry!" the people cried.

Finally the men emerged. As the last one came out the tilting shifted and groaned again. The men needed no more warning. They fled helter-skelter down the stairs, round and round. One stumbled and fell and almost went over the edge. He got up quickly and ran. As they turned the last bend by the common room the tilting groaned again. Slowly, almost imperceptibly at first, it leaned. The seaward wall crumpled under the pressure. The tilting fell gracefully, rapidly gathering speed until, with a deafening roar, it fell into the forest and exploded into a thousand pieces.

47 – Death of a King

The tiltings sat on a forest path waiting for morning. They'd moved away from the fallen building and its stench. They lit bonfires to keep themselves warm and ward off the darkness. The forest was quiet, as quiet as if the silencers were floating in the sky. A few slept peacefully, trusting in the wonderworks of Mia's friends.

"Can a man have babies?" a child asked Alf, pointing to Cam. Beer bellies were a complete novelty in Instar.

Alf grinned. "No," he said. "There's a strange drink where we come from. If you drink too much then you act silly and your belly swells like you're pregnant."

The child's eyes opened in wonder.

"Why do they do that?"

Alf shrugged.

The child giggled. "Can I poke his tummy?" he asked. "Will it burst?"

"I think you'd better not," said Alf. "You never know with Cam. He might laugh, or he might explode all over you. That would be really horrible!"

Alf got up and went to Siggy. The battle was still running through his mind and he was wide awake. "We came just in time," he said.

"I knew it'd be close," said Siggy. "Those cockroaches are clever. It was only a matter of time before they worked out how to bring down the tilting."

Mia came over and joined them.

"We are going to try to join a new community," she said. "We can't stay out here. We're too exposed."

"That won't work," said Siggy. "They'll attack again and again until they find our weakness or we run out of weapons."

"But Cam thought he'd hit the cockroach king with his gun," said Mia. "Perhaps he's dead."

"Dead or not, they'll come back till we're gone," said Siggy. "Think about it: they don't have a choice if they're going to gain control again."

Mia looked unhappy. "So what do we do?"

"We have a plan," said Alf. "But let's rest and await the morning. Then we'll discuss it with everybody."

A short while later the silencers floated into the sky. They looked so peaceful and beautiful that those still awake began to relax. Soon only the guards were pacing round and round the group, stoking the fires and keeping them bright.

***

'Keeee kee-reee! Keeee kee-reee!' cried the lilting yellow and red birds as the sun appeared. 'Keeee kee-reee! Keeee kee-reee!' Their call awakened the group. The men looked tired, but thankful to be alive. The children were subdued and the mothers quiet. Many were holding back tears. Mama went among them and soothed their fears. Her lack of fear communicated itself to others and gave them courage.

"We have a plan," said Farlin when the meeting had been called. "We are going to ask all the fighters from the neighboring tiltings to come with us and root out the Golden Ones once and for all. There'll be no peace or life worth living until they're gone."

The group stayed silent. Farlin was merely speaking what they'd already realized.

"We won't reveal our plan until the fighters are in place," said Jhek. "There have been traitors and turncoats. But first we must find a tilting to take in the women and children who cannot fight."

"I need strong men to come with me," said Alf. "We have to scavenge what weapons we can find, and go back to the portal tree to gather equipment."

"And I need speedy runners," said Siggy. "We must gather our strength."

Again there was silent assent. Ten men went with Alf, and eight youths and young men with Siggy and the rest headed down the path until they came to the neighboring tilting. Farlin knocked on the gate.

"Go away," called a voice. "We are not fighting. We are loyal to the Golden Ones in their wisdom and guidance."

"We have children needing shelter," said Farlin.

"Your children will bring death," came the answer. "Go away."

Farlin didn't argue further, but turned and walked to the next tilting. There they found a score of men ready and waiting for them.

"Siggy told us of the battle that's to come," they said. "We will join, but the rest wish to stay and we cannot force them."

"We'll take who we can, and grateful," said Farlin, and they continued on their way.

The next tilting was burned out and blackened. The wall had been undermined and bodies lay on the burnt out fires or strewn about.

"Those carrion," said Farlin of the Golden Ones, "they care for nothing but their precious gold."

Finally they came to Farlin's home, Sandler tilting, and were let in. They'd seen the burning of their neighbor and the toppling of Clairuz the previous night. They knew they were marked for they'd been surrounded and watched for the last few nights. Children, nursing mothers and old folk stayed and all the able bodied men and women joined Farlin as they made their way to the pyramid.

"Now that's a pile of gold," said Cam when he caught sight of the pyramid shining in the sunlight. "And all pure gold, you say?"

"Yes," said Farlin. "Think of it, Cam, if you got your hands on that building you'd be the richest person in your world, and then some."

"I'm thinking, I'm thinking," said Cam, licking his lips. "Trouble is, there's no way to carry it all home."

It was well into the afternoon by the time they reached the wall around the pyramid. All the gates were closed. Alf and his crew were already there, under the trees a few hundred yards from the gate. They were wearing masks over their mouths and pouring powder into small plastic bags and tying them to fireworks. Beside them were bulging backpacks and on the path lay metal tipped spears, swords and knives scavenged from the guards who had died in the fight.

"Over here, lads," said Cam, walking towards the gate. "Dig under the gate piers, both of them."

They'd hardly started digging when a guard looked over the wall. "What are you doing?" he shouted.

Cam stared at him for a moment. "Digging for worms," he said.

The guard looked around and saw the rest of the group scattered about. "Get back to your tiltings," he commanded. "The Garden of the Golden Ones is closed and forbidden. The Most High One will—"

His words were cut off as a golden slug knocked him out of sight. Cam had thrown it. "Take that to your High One. Tell him to put it where it hurts."

The diggers continued their efforts, but within minutes they heard guards gathering behind the gate.

Farlin sent a young man up a tree.

"How many, and what are they doing?" he asked.

"Dozens," was the reply. "And more are coming, all armed."

"Dig quickly, lads, and make a hole directly in the pillar," said Cam, and the diggers redoubled their efforts.

The guards hurled stones, slugs and spears over the wall. Men rushed to protect the diggers with shields. A few were hit and had to be dragged away, bleeding.

Various groups began to come in from the other tiltings, some accompanied by one of Siggy's runners. Most were young men and women armed with shovels and sharpened stakes. It wasn't a rousing sight. They stared at Cam's belly and his t-shirt streaked with sweat and dirt. He was holding a woven shield over his head and directing the diggers.

The Instars fought back, tossing stones and slugs and attacking any guard who showed his face over the wall. After last night's battle this skirmish seemed minor. The guards could not effectively attack, but neither could those outside the gate.

Finally Siggy and a few runners arrived. They were panting heavily.

"We've told all the tiltings that could make it here in time," said Siggy to Farlin. "The rest are too far away. I sent runners further afield. Perhaps fresh fighters will appear when we need them most." He looked around at the gathered group. "Is this all?" he asked.

"It's the best we have ... unless you have a better idea."

Fifteen minutes later the diggers were finished and Cam sent them back to the forest.

"All done," he shouted at Alf. "Get the mite."

Holding a shield over his head Alf ran in with a package for Cam. Then he darted into the hole beside the other pillar and worked frantically as stones and slugs pounded on his shield.

"Are you ready?" said Cam when he was done.

"Ready as I'll ever be," said Alf.

The Darkling Beasts

Cam looked at Siggy and Farlin. They gave a thumbs-up.

"Right then," shouted Cam in his booming voice. "Stand back! Stand back! Get behind the trees."

Everyone backed off to the edge of the forest.

"Now," said Cam to Alf.

Cam flicked his lighter. The flame went out. "Drat," he said, flicking it again.

"Run, Cam, run!" screamed Alf who was already up and fleeing.

Cam flicked his lighter a third time. No good. And again. This time it lit and he held it under the fuse. The fuse smoldered, then caught. Up jumped Cam and ran for his life as guards looked over the wall and wondered what was happening. Cam didn't get far. Alf's dynamite exploded with a huge boom and Cam was bowled over. He lay still and didn't move. Then the second explosion shook the ground. Pieces of wall rocketed into the heights and dirt and dust filled the air. The whole gate collapsed inwards and the guards were decimated.

The Instars were too shocked to move. They'd been told that there would be an explosion, but never in their wildest dreams had they imagined this.

Alf and Siggy raced towards Cam as soon as the debris had fallen.

"Are you okay?" shouted Alf, shaking him.

"What?" said Cam, slowly sitting up.

"Are you okay?" shouted Alf and Siggy together.

Cam shook is head. "I can't hear," he shouted back. "I'm stone deaf."

He looked around and saw the Instars slowly come out of the forest.

"Well, don't just stand there," he commanded. "Get in! Get in!"

Jhek came to his senses first. "Charge!" he cried, and the men and women found their feet and charged for the gaping hole in the wall with spears and spades at the ready. They didn't get any resistance. Most of the guards lay dead or wounded, and the rest were running for the pyramid. Some Instars ran after them.

"Stop," cried Siggy. "Stick together," and they stopped and waited.

They marched up to the pyramid. Already the late afternoon light had turned to reddish-orange. Guard animals challenged them but quickly kept their distance when a few well thrown spears killed a couple. They gathered from all over the grounds and formed a pack that circled the group. They shifted colors from black to red and back again. Finally Cam walked out to meet them and let loose both barrels of his shotgun when they approached, thinking him an easy target. They howled and fled as buckshot tore into their flesh.

The Instars went on and stopped short of the main entrance. The doors were closed and guards were looking out the window openings on the upper floors. A few began to throw slugs, but suddenly stopped, as if by command.

"Break up! Break up!" commanded Cam, and three groups ran around the building to bar and jam the other three doors. After a while most came back while others stayed to make sure the doors remained shut.

"None of us saw any guards outside," said Farlin. "They must all be inside the pyramid."

"That's good," said Cam, taking three bound sticks of dynamite from his pack.

"My turn," said Siggy. "You're too dangerous."

"What?" said Cam, holding his hand to his ear.

"Never mind," said Siggy, pulling the dynamite out of his hands and bolting towards the doors.

The guards at the windows hesitated, then a sudden rain of slugs came down, but Siggy was already safe and hidden in the recess. Everyone backed off and took cover as Siggy jammed the dynamite under the central pair of double doors. He lit the fuse, and ran zigzagging away from the building. Counting out loud he flung himself to the ground and covered his ears just as he reached ten.

Boom! went the dynamite, and shards of gold flew spinning and whining through the air. When the smoke cleared, the doors lay twisted and torn like tin foil. The Instars rushed into the pyramid. The guards on the lower level were shocked and concussed in the confined space and were quickly killed or routed up to the next level. Taking the stairs proved more difficult. Spears and slugs rained down on them. Three people were killed and others injured.

"Stop fighting," cried Cam. "Pull back."

Everyone pulled back from the stairs. Outside, evening was falling; inside it was getting dark.

"It's time for the rockets," said Alf.

The Darkling Beasts

"What?" asked Cam.

"Rockets," shouted Siggy. "Rockets."

"Ah, rockets," shouted Cam back at him. "I'm beginning to hear again. Let's try. Nothing ventured, nothing gained."

"Cover your mouths with cloth," Siggy told the group. "This stuff won't kill you, but you'll want to breathe as little as possible."

They stacked woven shields on the floor and stuck three large rockets into the weave. The rockets were carefully wrapped with plastic bags held in place with rubber bands. When they were ready Farlin addressed the group in a whisper.

"When these rockets fly up and explode the whole space will be filled with fumes. Then we'll rush the stairs and take the next floor. If we are pushed back, I will signal and we will all retreat together. Hold your shields over you on the stairs. Got it?"

Everyone nodded their heads.

Alf and Siggy and Mia lit the rockets and others pushed the whole contraption into the stairwell with their spears. Golden slugs rained down, but too late. The three rockets took off with a whoosh one after the other. They heard one bounce off a wall and then, an instant later, explode. The other two kept going and with two loud booms burst high up in the stairwell. The smell of fireworks filled the air. Before anyone could rush the stairs an ungodly clamor stopped them in their tracks. It sounded as if all the guards, every single one of them, were shouting, crying, screaming, wailing, coughing, choking and moaning. The Instars looked at each other in terror, not knowing whether to flee the monster they'd unleashed or stand and hold their ground.

Suddenly, guards came tumbling down the stairs, followed by others crawling rapidly on hands and knees. The Instars backed up and stared as the guards writhed and foamed at the mouth. Finally they went into spasms which slowly faded away and they were still. Slowly the great noise abated. Only wretched coughing and the sound of writhing remained. Then there was silence.

A young woman came rushing in from outside.

"What happened?" she cried. "The guards were flinging themselves out the windows by the dozens. Those that survived the fall died writhing and twitching."

"Looks like your mum was on to something," said Alf, patting Cam on the back.

"Amazing," said Cam. "Just amazing. That roach killer is something else."

"Let's go upstairs to the sanctum and see if it works there as well," said Siggy.

They climbed the stairs, Farlin insisting that they check each floor as they went. None were alive. The pyramid was littered with hundreds of guards, every one of them twisted and contorted.

"How many of them are there?" asked Jhek in wonder. "We never saw this many guards."

"We never saw this many guards *together*," said Mia. "None of us could tell them apart. I think we were seeing different guards all the time but thought they were the same ones."

They came to the threshold. The golden doors were closed. By now it was too dark to see properly and flashlights had been turned on.

Cam stood in wonder before the doors. "By my warts," he said. "Look at them swingers. They're beautiful! Don't tell me roaches made these?"

"No," said Mia. "I think there really were Golden Ones, many, many years ago; so long ago that we cannot remember. They are the ones who built the pyramid."

Farlin went to the doors and pulled on one. It was locked. He glanced about. The Guards of the Golden Door, the highest rank, were lying about at the bottom of the short flight of steps before the threshold. They'd died without leaving their post. Bits and pieces of rocket paper and plastic were scattered about and the acrid smell of gunpowder and insecticide hung in the air. He went down the stairs and searched the highest ranking guard. He found a chain and key around his neck. He returned to the doors.

Farlin slid the key into the keyhole and turned. The mechanism, thousands of years old, worked smoothly and flawlessly.

"Wait," said Siggy. "I have an idea." He took out two cone-shaped insecticide bombs from a pack and stood before the doors. "Just open it a crack and close it again," he said, and lit the bombs. Dense yellow smoke began to billow from their tops and Siggy held them away from himself.

Farlin pulled on the heavy door. It moved a fraction but didn't open. He gripped the handle and pulled with all his might. The door opened

The Darkling Beasts

with a tearing sound. The edges had been sealed with a sticky substance. Loud hisses and clicks sounded inside and cockroach legs and feelers reached out for Siggy. Siggy tossed the bombs inside and jumped back as Farlin slammed the door shut and turned the key.

A great scurrying and rustling was heard, followed by rasps and squeals. A moment later a shout went up outside. Everyone ran to the windows. The sun was golden red in its final minutes and there was still light to see by. They looked up. Panels were swinging open all over the upper pyramid, golden panels no one knew were there. Out of them poured scores of flying cockroaches, huge ones. A great stench went up. A few flew erratically towards the forest but most began to fly in crazy circles, buzzing loudly and crashing against the pyramid or plummeting to the ground. The fighters below ran and speared them, but soon realized that they were dying anyway and stood back to watch. Lastly, at the tip of the pyramid, a panel swung open and the largest cockroach flew out. He was twelve feet long and had a wingspan of twenty. He was hideous, but with a beautiful, deep, golden color that caught and glowed in the last rays of the sun. He flew upwards in spirals above the pointed peak of the pyramid. Round and round he went, as if reaching for the sun itself, his wings sheer and transparent and of purest gold. Cam raised his shotgun and let both barrels fly. The king's wings shredded and he fell, striking the point of the pyramid and tumbling down the sides to the lawn below. In a moment the fighters were upon him, sticking him full of spears.

"Bloody bug," said Cam, breaking his shotgun and throwing away the shells before the sun winked out.

48 – *Night at the Pyramid*

They spent the night in the pyramid. The mood was upbeat, and even though the howls and noises sounded from the forest they were diminished and no animal or beast appeared. Of the guards, none were seen. Sometime after midnight the silencers rose into the air and a hush descended. Everyone, except for the night watch, slept.

'Teee-la, teee-la,' called the teela birds flying round and round Golden Hill when the sun emerged.

'Keeee kee-reee! Keeee kee-reee!' called the quick flying yellow and red birds speeding between the trees. More and more birds flew around the pyramid. They seemed happier and freer today and finally massed into a great flock that swirled and dipped in unison.

"That's the strangest sun," said Cam, shading his eyes and looking up at the small speck glowing red through the morning mist.

"Yours is stranger to me," said Farlin, standing next to him.

"I suppose," said Cam. "But to me, yours seems stuck."

"Our sun is the eternal center of the universe," said Farlin. "When I saw how your sun moved I felt dizzy and not able to find myself."

Alf and Mia came over with Siggy.

"Siggy says we have to search the whole pyramid thoroughly," said Mia.

"And why is that?" asked Cam.

"No eggs," said Siggy. "All we see are adults. If we don't find their brooding ground they'll just come back."

Farlin looked surprised. He hadn't thought of that. He called everyone over and soon a crew was clearing out the pyramid and dragging the guard's bodies to the forest to be burned. Others were sent to tell the tiltings what had happened during the night and to come and collect food from the fields.

A separate group hefted their weapons and began to search the pyramid from top to bottom. The lower levels were soon covered. These levels were so well known, so worked over and laboriously scraped by the Instars that they knew every inch of the place. The leaders entered the Golden Sanctuary and turned on their flashlights. The pesticide bombs lay on the floor where Siggy had thrown them, the partly burned labels saying: Lively's Guaranteed Cockroach Cruncher. A dozen roaches lay on their backs, but most seemed to have made their way outside. They searched the entry room, everyone marveling at the intricate relief work covering the walls and ceiling. The walls showed large scenes with groups of figures elegantly but simply dressed, all with calm, harmonious faces, yet with personality. The ceiling had symbols or diagrams showing, to Alf and Siggy's eyes, a set of solar systems and their relationships.

The Darkling Beasts

"Listen," said Siggy.

No one heard what he was talking about.

"The door," said Siggy. "Listen."

Then they heard it: a soft whoosh. It was slowly gathering strength, and soon a faint whistle could be heard. Siggy pulled a threshold door open. The sound stopped but the air moved upwards in a cool rush.

"The pyramid is warming up and acting like a chimney," said Siggy. "It must be because the panels are open above us. Jam the doors."

They began to push a door open when Siggy stopped them.

"I doubt the real Golden Ones used brute force," he said, running his hands over the panels. He reached up and touched the center of the sun in the door. It swung open by itself and stayed. Farlin touched the sun in the other door and it too swung open. Light and fresh air poured into the sanctum and soon it felt like a thousand years of mustiness was being washed away.

"Well, what do you know," said Siggy, pointing to the inside of one door.

Everyone stared at it, unsure of what he was looking at. Siggy pointed to the focal point of the lower panel: a tree on a hill. The tree was hollow, for you could see into a natural opening like an inverted 'V' at the bottom of the trunk.

"It looks like our tree," said Alf, "or one just like it."

"And it's on a door," said Siggy. "Very appropriate."

Below the tree was a short tunnel leading into another scene. It showed a round, outwardly curved earth and a series of sun positions as it moved across the sky. There was a moon too, going through it's phases, and the sky was filled with stars.

"That's the earth," said Siggy. "There's the big dipper in the sky. And look, an arrow is pointing to Alkaid, the last star on the handle."

They searched further, moving down the hallways. Cam's eyes widened as he saw the piles of golden slugs filling the rooms.

"Take what you want," said Farlin, laughing. "They'll just weigh you down, though."

"Later," said Cam, wiping his mouth. "Later. I could do with more weight of this kind."

They went up the stairs to the next level. Here a couple of exterior panels were open, the roaches having had the time to activate them. All the walls were covered with symbols and writing, and Siggy stared at them intently, trying to decipher them, but much was hidden behind the detritus. So it was for floor after floor until they climbed the final stairs. It was narrow, only wide enough for two abreast. One panel stood open and let the light and air in. This was the one the king used to go on his final flight. They found the cables crudely welded to the walls and the pile of bones in the corner. Food trays with dried meals were scattered about.

Mia came last up the stairs, holding Alf's hand. Everyone turned to her. She looked about, her eyes sad and fragile.

"Here's where I was chained," she said, walking over and kicking the golden cable. She pointed upwards to the king's nest. "That's were he lived."

Farlin climbed up and looked about the apex room. It was empty except for the foul nest upon the altar.

Alf led Mia over to the open panel and let her look out. The sill was low and the fresh air and view revived her. The wind in the room was brisk and ruffled their hair. Siggy was not tall enough to see out properly and Farlin lifted him up. He glanced out for a moment, but wasn't interested and hopped down.

"It's got to be here somewhere," he said.

"What?" asked Farlin.

"The hatchery," said Siggy, exasperated. "That's why we're searching this place so carefully."

He turned to Cam.

"Where do cockroaches breed? I've never read about them."

"Damp, warm, dark places," said Cam.

"The upper pyramid was dark, but not warm at night and certainly not damp," said Siggy. "It can't be here. Is there nothing you remember that might help?" he asked Mia.

"No, I've told you everything," she said. "It was dark and I wasn't here long."

"Let's go to the ground floor," said Siggy. "We missed something."

49 – Brooding Ground

The pyramid was quickly being cleaned up. Folk poured in from the surrounding tiltings to gape and stare. When they'd had their fill, they helped out. Already crews were in the fields harvesting crops. Men with spears were searching the grounds to clear them of the guard animals. They also brought along slingshots, a weapon Siggy had shown them how to make. As yet their aim was hopeless.

Siggy paced systematically back and forth through the ground floor of the lower pyramid. Alf and Mia walked beside him.

"We're not sure what you're looking for," said Mia, timidly.

Siggy was in a temper.

"How am I to know what I'm looking for?" he demanded, his hunchback seeming hunchier than ever. "Somewhere, somehow, there's a way to another section, another whole complex."

He paused.

"A bunker," he said. "It might be a bunker. Have you never seen where they bred or laid their eggs? No sign at all? Did you never wonder where they came from?"

"No," said Mia in a small voice. She felt stupid not seeing anything.

"Farlin! Farlin!" shouted Siggy, marching over to him. "Does no one know anything? What the hell were you all doing while this was going on?"

Alf took Mia's arm and led her away. "It's best to avoid him when he's in a tizzy. He'll cool off as soon as he gets a lead. He hates not knowing."

They went and sat on the outside steps. It was warm and Mia rested her head on Alf's shoulder.

"Did you really never see anything odd?" asked Alf. "Something out of place, or different, even if it seemed harmless."

"Don't you start," said Mia, sitting up and giving Alf a clout. "I told you, no."

She rested her head back onto his shoulder and sighed.

"Wait a minute," she said, sitting up. "Once, when I was only seven or so, I was late leaving the pyramid. I'd been scraping for hours and forgot the time. Suddenly a guard appeared and ordered me out. He kept shouting at me, but also shouted down the hall in an unknown language. I left the room I was in and saw that I was alone and the last to leave. I was terrified. I ran through the lower level and out the door. As I passed the stairs I saw guards. They looked like all the guards did, but there was something new about them. They stood peering about as if they'd never seen the place before. And they smelled different, or at least I assumed it was them. They smelled organic and musty—earthy. Then I ran out the door and barely made it to the nearest tilting before dark. My parents spent the night in fear that I'd been killed."

Alf jumped up. "Siggy, Siggy," he called. "The stairs. It's by the stairs."

Siggy stopped pacing and looked over. He brightened into a huge smile and whacked his head. "Well, of course it's by the stairs. Where else would you locate stairs? Duh!"

He ran to the bottom of the first flight and examined it carefully. Nothing. He got down and peered at the joints where the floor met the riser. Nothing. He crawled on his hands and knees over the floor at the bottom of the stairwell. There was not much to see, just the pattern of rectangular, golden flagstones found on all the floors. Siggy examined each joint carefully.

"It's around here somewhere," he said to the crowd that had gathered. "Farlin, stamp your feet across the bottom of the stairwell. Everyone else keep quiet," and he lay with his ear to the floor.

A hush fell and Farlin slowly stamped across step by step. Siggy heard a faint echo.

"It's here, below," he said. "Now, how do we get in? There must be a touch panel or lever, something."

Everyone searched high and low, pushing and pulling, hitting and stamping every surface and corner. But there wasn't much to see. The wall, stairs and floor were simple in the extreme.

"Stop," said Siggy. "Everyone stop."

Everyone stopped.

"Think," said Siggy. "Somewhere around here there is one place which is slightly more worn, or slightly dirtier, or slightly cleaner or slightly smoother than the rest. That's where they pushed or pulled to open a door to the lower levels. Look for it."

The Darkling Beasts

Everyone gazed around, searching every surface for a sign of difference, but there was none. The floor and stairs showed no sign of wear at all, as if the gold had been mixed into an alloy and made as hard as diamonds.

"It can't be located where someone could accidently touch it, poke it or step on it," said Siggy. "Somewhere out of easy reach."

Alf looked over to Mia. She stood with her head down and eyes closed. Suddenly she smiled.

"I know," she said.

She grabbed a spear from a man's hand and raced up the stairs. Round and round she went, up and up, as the crowd below watched. Finally she reached the top.

"Stand back below," she called.

She reached up with the spear and lightly touched the central globe of the sun motif on the ceiling.

Far below, a section of the floor slid noiselessly downward and rotated away. There were the stairs. They fell downwards in a spiral, with landings at regular intervals. The rest was in darkness. A dank, moist odor rose upwards, smelling of earth and leaf mold. A soft rustling and scurrying was heard below. There was life in there.

"Told you," shouted Mia. "I saw a guard up here once near closing. He had a long golden staff in his hand. It didn't make sense at the time."

Siggy made a move to go down the stairs.

"Wait," cried Mia. "You don't know what's down there. Throw one of your smoke bombs in first and I'll close the door again."

A moment later, Alf and Siggy lit two bombs and tossed them in. Cam threw down a few bangers wrapped with roach killer for good measure. Mia touch the globe. As the floor rotated back the bangers exploded, the sound reverberating upwards. Those who had come after the battle leaped backwards in fright. From below came a rising hue and cry, as if from hell. The floor panel stopped and rose. It slipped seamlessly into place with a slight thud, cutting short the clamor in mid stream.

They waited; then sorted out their weapons and lights and Mia opened the floor panel again. A different smell rose up this time. It was deadly quiet.

Suddenly a sob was heard, human and young. Mama grabbed a flashlight from Farlin and led the way down. She called out and voices replied. Far below they found the recently abducted girls locked in a number of rooms.

50 – Octahedron

Below ground was another pyramid, an inversion of the one above: the same size, the same shape and the same number of levels. It too came to a point, with the last seven levels being the inner sanctum. Here they found the queen in the final room and apex. The doors of the lower sanctum had been open when the bombs were dropped in. She was still lying in a foul nest, her body huge, soft and golden, her sides bloated with eggs. Many eggs had been squeezed out in her death throes and they covered the nest and floor in long slimy rows.

The floors immediately above were converted for brooding the eggs. The rooms were layered with vegetable matter four feet thick and covered with leaves. No one knew what this meant until Siggy dug down with a spear. It was surprisingly warm underneath, like a compost heap. Siggy extracted an egg, about six inches long. It was still alive, a form wriggling inside a translucent casing. They opened it and out came a partly formed, milky white grub.

Further up, some of the eggs were hatched. Inside a mature egg they found a whitish cockroach with a golden sheen to its skin. It squirmed out of Alf's hands, leaped onto the compost and scurried under the leaves. They pushed the leaves aside and found it, but already it was dying from the insecticide. They found others under the leaves too, all dead. They'd tried to escape the fumes by digging into the litter.

The next levels had food storage, water, liquids in large clay jars, and the like. Unlike the other floors there were a number of openings in the perimeter walls. They were rough, about six feet wide, and lacked the finesse of the original builders. They led into underground tunnels. Nothing could be seen in them, or at least as far as their lights shone. Finally they came upon a tunnel which gave a clue as to their use. A huge grub, dark skinned and clawed, with black globular eyes, fierce mandibles and a two foot long proboscis of hardest keratin lay partly out of the tunnel. Its whole front section was hard and plated and patterned with a web of dark, geometric lines. The rear end was soft and leathery. This was one of those that lived beneath the forest floor and created the terrible noises. After that, even though they doubted any grubs would come near the strong, lingering smell of insecticide, they posted guards to give warning in case another of these beasts showed up.

The next floor had something stranger. In room after room hung large, oblong sacks from the ceilings. To Alf and Siggy they looked for all the world like pupas. In some rooms the sacks had split open, their silver-gray skins hanging empty and dull; in other rooms, piles of sacks had been cut from the ceiling and left in the corner. The pupas were eerie, hanging in neat, organized rows, as still as death. Cam poked one and the dark form inside moved.

"Cut it open," said Siggy.

Cam slit the sack from top to bottom with a hunting knife in one rapid motion. Out tumbled a naked human form, male but sexless, with limbs and head but only a vaguely defined face. The eyes, however, were still those of the grub, large and black and bulbous. Guard's eyes.

The body squirmed on the floor and mewed until Farlin stuck it through. "So this is where the guards come from," he said, and he went about the room thrusting his spear into each hanging sack.

After that all the rooms on this level were searched and the sacks dispatched. On the levels directly below the upper pyramid were the guard's living quarters, with housing, sleeping, feeding and maintenance well defined and organized. There was a clear hierarchy, with bunk beds in many rooms and an officer's quarters. Lastly, there was a single, comfortable room for the chief guard.

* * *

The next few days were busy. They sealed up the tunnels into the pyramid and cleaned out the whole building. The wall and gate were repaired, or at least as well as they were able, for they didn't have the technology of the Golden Ones. The Instars buried their dead and attended to chores long overdue. It was a rollercoaster ride of high joy and sorrow, anger and release. Ester and Farlin and their extended family were often seen together at meal times or when people rested. For them it was a time of joy, mostly, though Farlin and Ester wished their parents were still alive to share their happiness at finding each other.

Hunting groups went about, seeking out the giant grubs in the forest. They were led by a self-appointed Cam who declared that he was the man for the job and told tales of daring-do from his war days which were hard to believe but impressed some of the women. First they located the telltale signs of the grubs under the forest floor, and using long rakes they pulled and disturbed the leaf litter. If the grub rose up and grabbed the rake, a dozen spears, their points dipped in insecticide, pierced it through. Then it roared and fled, or rose out of the ground, writhing in its death agony. They dispatched hundreds this way in the first few days. Then it became harder to find the beasts by day for they were intelligent and communicated with each other and refused to surface. Cam had stout cages built in which four men sat during the night with poisoned spears sticking out. They made noise and attracted the grubs to them and killed them that way. Soon this ceased being effective and the beasts even stopped howling at night.

One group, led by Cam, decided to hunt within the tunnels. This was dangerous, but effective. First they fumigated a section and discovered a whole network underneath the forest. They also found that the tunnels were used by wingless roaches who dug smaller side burrows. These were predatory roaches, with fierce, razor-sharp mandibles and a screeching, clicking voice. After a few days, however, all the main passages around the pyramid were blocked with dirt and which proved too awkward to dig out. Cam reckoned that sooner or later the grubs would die, or have to pupate and turn into guards. Then they'd starve in their tunnels, or come out and be tracked down and killed. Even if it took a while they now had no way of breeding and were doomed. Likewise for the predatory roaches, for they were all female but infertile.

Siggy spent days wandering about the pyramid trying to decipher the friezes in the inner sanctum. The walls and ceilings in the inverted pyramid were mostly destroyed and defaced, but not in the inner sanctum of the queen. There, as above, they were still intact, except they were inverted. Rather than the figures standing out from the wall, they were hollowed into the wall, like the negative form of a mold. It made a curious impression on Siggy after he'd spent some time with them. Down below, he had the feeling that the space about him was being sculpted and shaped through a drawing, sectional action, whereas in the upper sanctum, the friezes impressed themselves on him, like a hand pushing on clay.

A great meeting was called. All who where able came to Golden Hill. It was a beautiful day and Mia told Alf it was lucky the first winds of the stormy season had not begun. Perhaps this would be the last time for them to meet outside until the calm season came. The Instars divided up the tasks of farming, gardening, food preserving, weaving, building and blacksmithing into groups of tiltings. Each group had a set of tasks which occupied them for most of the year, but also a free time when their duties were light or nonexistent. A separate group was created from the more adventurous ones, mostly the young men, to hunt down the grubs, roaches and animals which had been bred to kill people.

***

Siggy took Alf and Mia around the pyramid the next day. He led them through the upper and lower sanctuary. By now some of the pellets had been hauled out of the rooms and the beauty of the walls was even more apparent.

"So what do the pictures say?" asked Mia.

"I think much of it is the history of the real Golden Ones and a record of their time here," said Siggy. "You can see how one person, a leader perhaps, appears for a while and then is gone." He led them into a room. "Look, this is a fighter queen. See her spear in one hand and a globe in the other. Her foot is resting on some sort of creature, but nothing we've ever seen."

Mia looked carefully at the creature. "That's a fandex," she said with certainty. "We have stories about them and they describe them just like this. See, they have eyes with vertical slits and skin which is covered with small bumps. I bet that's Queen Findling."

They looked around some more.

"And here's another place," said Siggy. "They seem to be building machines of some sort. They look like they could fly, though not like an airplane. See all the symbols in this room. I think they were leaving instructions or knowledge, but I can't find the key."

Siggy took them back to the great threshold doors. "This is the clearest place for me," he said. "I think the Golden Ones found or created a way through to our world."

"Then how come we don't have Golden Ones?" asked Alf.

"How do you know we don't, or didn't?" said Siggy. "The ancient

Egyptian culture arose overnight and they built massive pyramids too, every bit as clever as this one."

Alf nodded. "At least we don't have cockroaches," he said, "or not like the ones here."

Siggy gave him a look. "Are you sure?" he asked, but Alf couldn't answer one way or the other.

"There's one other thing I don't get," said Siggy. "How the cockroaches took over without the Instars knowing about it. Is there nothing in your myths, Mia?"

"I don't think so," she said. "We always thought the Golden Ones were here and never left."

"But there must have been a change," said Alf.

"If there was it's not spoken of. We never saw the cockroaches or grubs or their connection to the guards. The old legends speak of how generous the Golden Ones were, how they taught us to make tiltings and cultivate the plants and do blacksmithing. And the guards also told us how powerful but kind the Golden Ones behind the doors were and how they kept us fed and safe from harm. The Golden Ones had always kept themselves separate and never mixed with the ordinary people. Not a single Golden One is said to have married an Instar, ever—except for the last queen. We were different races and too far apart."

Siggy didn't seem satisfied, but kept quiet. He knelt down by the threshold door and looked carefully at the relief. "Well, well, what do you know," he said. "Come look at this."

Alf and Mia bent down and looked where Siggy was pointing. There, where the passage led from Instar to the earth world, was another tunnel leading off. It was smaller and led downwards towards the bottom of the door.

"See this small tunnel," said Siggy, pointing, "I hadn't noticed it before because the tunnel looks like part of the frame that contains the relief, but it's not," and he traced his finger down the groove until it stopped. Then it looked like the tunnel had been plugged. After that the tunnel continued and went underneath the door.

"The story goes on," said Siggy in surprise, running his fingers beneath the door. "There are shapes here too. We have to take this door off its hinges."

They rounded up some of the stronger men who took the weight off the door as Alf slid the pins out of the hinges. The door was lowered to the floor. Underneath they found that the tunnel led to a hollowed out space within the door itself. It wasn't very deep, only five inches or so. It was filled with perfectly cast and exquisitely detailed roaches, grubs, eggs and sacks. At the very end were two large roaches. One was clearly the queen for she was larger and had eggs in rows on her flanks. The king lay over a young woman.

51 – Winds of Change

A storm came, the first of the season. The forest swayed and leaves shook free. Branches flew through the air, and rain blew in the window openings of the pyramid. Most of the people from the Nova tilting had been staying at the pyramid and they'd become the de facto caretakers of it and the grounds. They'd spread themselves out wherever it suited them. Now some went to the upper section where the panels kept the rain and wind out. Others went below into the old guard rooms and quickly found that being under the earth kept the temperature cool but even.

The next day thick mist enveloped the world until midday. When it cleared people sat out in the sun or went about their jobs. Alf and Mia were walking along one of the paths that ran through the meadows.

"You'll have to build another tilting," said Alf. "I'd love to see one going up."

"We can't build until the dry season comes," said Mia. "The tilting juice has to dry completely before it's waterproof and strong enough to bear weight properly. And besides, they take a long time to build. Some grow for years."

"Why don't you come back with us?" said Alf. "We can't stay much longer. Cam has to sort out his business and my parents will be beginning to wonder if I'm ever coming home."

"You can always come back," said Mia.

"That's true," agreed Alf.

He hesitated.

"Come with us, Mia. It'd be an adventure for you—and like you said, you can always come back."

"I've had adventure enough," said Mia quietly. "Besides, there's plenty to be done here. A whole new world is opening up for us. We can even relearn how to build boats and see if we can fish. Perhaps we'll find other lands. There had to be a reason for the roaches not wanting us to explore."

Cam happened by with Ester, Siggy and another woman who'd been hanging around Cam whenever she could. Her name was Shanting.

"Well, kiddo," said Cam to Alf, "Siggy wants to go back and I hear you do too. I've collected as much gold as I can carry so let's be off this afternoon."

"What's the rush?" said Shanting, taking his arm. "You've still got lots to teach us about metal work."

Cam blushed. "Oh, but I am coming back, never fear," he said, looking Shanting in the eyes.

Mia glanced at Alf and tried to hide a grin.

"In fact, I'll be back tomorrow," said Cam. "I have to see that my mum's taken care of, that's all. She'll be set up for life with a load of gold."

Ester laughed. "She will have more than enough, and to spare. I'd love to see her face when she finds out that you're the hero of Instar."

Cam blushed again and looked at his shoes. "'Twas nothing. Just doing what I must."

"What about you?" Mia asked Ester.

Ester sighed. "I don't think I'll return," she said, "at least not for now. I'm needed here, much more than there."

"Are you sure you want to go back, Cam?" said Siggy. "There's going to be hell to pay if they work out that it was you who stole the dynamite and fireworks. Why not wait until it's forgotten."

"I left them both more than enough in gold," said Cam, indignantly. "I'm no thief."

"The police might not see it that way," said Alf.

Cam shrugged and didn't seem worried. Besides, once his mind was made up, that was that.

* * *

The Darkling Beasts

Alf and Siggy said their farewells and reassured everyone they'd be back soon. They filled their packs with gold and followed after Cam as he staggered ahead of them with Shanting at his side. They wound their way through the forest and past the remnants of Nova tilting. They'd just turned up the hill towards the hollow tree when Cam's pack burst with the weight it was carrying and the nuggets spilled onto the ground.

"Drats and dashes," said Cam, annoyed. "Never buy a cheap pack. It'll always let you down. When I was a marine we had packs build like tanks. They never gave out."

Shanting, however, seemed pleased. "Well, that takes care of it," she said. "You stay here and I'll fix that bag for you. In the end you'll be able to carry even more."

Cam flustered and mumbled, but didn't say no.

Siggy winked at Alf and Mia as they left the gold lying where it fell and continued up the hill. It was late afternoon and the sky was clear overhead, but on the horizon dark clouds had gathered and were beginning to boil. Another storm was in the making.

"We'll be back soon," said Alf, dropping into the passage. He took the packs from Siggy and lowered them down.

Siggy jumped into the hole beside Alf.

"What if the door won't open?" asked Mia, suddenly on the verge of tears.

"It's never closed for long," said Alf, giving her a hug, "or at least not so far."

"And Ester made us food," said Siggy cheerfully, "just in case we get hungry."

The boys waved goodbye and went down the passageway. They turned right and walked to the door. There were no new scratches. Alf pulled the handle. It opened, and Kitty-o ran mewing past them to Instar.

"So what's your rush?" said Siggy with a chuckle.

They wound their way through the maze and found the entry door open. They were in Cam's pole barn. In front of them was Cam's mum with her hands behind her back. With her were the police.

52 – Arrested

"We didn't steal nothing," said Siggy, looking the policewoman in the eye. "How many times do we have to tell you?"

Siggy and Alf were sitting in a police van and Siggy was annoyed. The police had been questioning them for an hour. They asked the same questions over and over again.

"Yes, we know Cam. Yes, the truck and Hall are his. Yes, we've helped him at carnivals. Yes, we know Cam's mum. Yes, we're staying with her. No, I don't know where Cam is. No, we can't remember when he parked the Hall truck in the barn."

Alf didn't like lying, but he had no choice. Siggy seemed not to be bothered one bit. Besides, if they'd told the whole truth they'd not be believed anyway. Outside, Cam's mum was giving a police officer hell. They could hear her screaming and telling the officer that her son was a purple heart marine and an outstanding member of society, and who were those dynamite people to be accusing him and concocting a fanciful story about lumps of gold, and if it was gold, and Cam had taken the dynamite, which he hadn't, then they'd be fully paid and then some, and didn't the policeman know that the Campbells were thieves and liars, and hadn't they been paid handsomely if the fireworks had been stolen, and it wasn't Cam who stole them anyway, and where would a carnival worker get lumps of gold the size of your fist, that's nonsense, and why was she, a woman of dignity, handcuffed without cause or charge on her own property? The officer replied, sounding weary, and eventually uncuffed her.

A policeman drove the truck and Hall out of the barn.

"Where are you taking that?" asked Siggy, suddenly worried.

The policewoman said they were impounding it as evidence. And besides, the license plates were out of date and Cam would have to turn up and pay the fee. Then they'd ask him a question or two.

Siggy felt it was time to end this whole thing. It was getting dark and he wanted to rest. He also didn't want the police to ask any more questions about where Alf was from, or himself for that matter. He had no ID at all.

"Waaa!" cried Siggy, suddenly throwing his head onto his arms and bawling his eyes out. "Waaa! Waaa! Waaa!"

Alf took the cue and started sniffling. "I don't want to go to jail," he sobbed. "I'm so scared. I just want to go back to Cam's mum and eat supper."

Cam's mum heard them crying and marched over.

"What are you doing with my babies?" she shouted, glaring at the policewoman. "Look what you've done, you monster! They're crying! A whole hour you've been questioning them. They need to go inside and have a solid meal. Are you really going to arrest them and send them to jail? They haven't done anything wrong. Arrest us now or let us go."

The policewoman let the boys out of the van and they walked towards the house.

They were almost there when the policewoman called out: "Boys, you forgot your backpacks," and lifted one up.

Her arms strained under the load.

"What have you got in here?" she asked, puzzled. "Let's have a look, shall we?"

* * *

Siggy and Alf sat in separate interrogation rooms at the police station. Two detectives had questioned them closely, but without much luck. Both of them said that the gold was theirs and that they hadn't stolen it. That was all they got out of them. The detectives sat in the corner office comparing notes.

"I had someone check the gold against the lumps that were left at the dynamite shed and at the Campbells," said Detective Sander to his colleague, Detective Fits. "They're the same. The Campbells suddenly changed their tune when they found out that the lumps really were gold and worth far more than what was stolen. They'd thought it was painted lead or something. Now they're refusing to press any charges and saying they're no longer sure it was Cam's truck they'd seen pulling away from their shed."

"Something's going on," said Detective Fits, "sure as I'm sitting here."

"I agree," said Detective Sander, "but with dynamite and kids involved, that makes it much more serious. Contributing to the delinquency of a minor and all that."

Detective Fits nodded. "Well, the boy's stories are the same, and it's not illegal to have gold, but no one ever walks around with this much."

Detective Sander chuckled. "That's for sure. It can't be theirs, but since we can't prove it—"

They were interrupted by a clerk.

"The information has come in: the Alf boy is who he says he is: Alfred Singworthy Upton-Hill. We tracked down his parents ... but it was kind of odd."

"What do you mean?" asked Detective Sander.

"They were delighted to hear that he was fine, but vague as to the date they'd last seen him. They were a little surprised that he was here in Upper Farnon. They said they'd gone to a carnival and thought he'd met friends. He often went off as he pleased and that's how they liked to bring him up, independent and free and all that."

"Parents," said Detective Fits, looking heavenward. "They should be outlawed or forced to take courses in proper parenting."

"And what about the other boy?" asked Detective Sander. "He's an odd one with his bare feet, red hair and hunchback."

"That's not his fault," said Detective Fits, annoyed.

"True," said Detective Sander. "I didn't mean to disparage him. He's as bright as a button, clear as day, but pretends to know nothing and be quite stupid and a crybaby. I don't believe it."

The clerk coughed.

"Oh, right, the information," said Detective Fits. "What did you find out about him?"

"Nothing," said the clerk. "Not a thing. There's no Siggy Upton-Hill, or Singular Elf Upton-Hill, and Alf's parents said there was no actual boy they knew of that name—though their son has had an imaginary companion of that name since he was little. Played with him all the time, apparently."

Detective Sander snorted. "Did you take fingerprints?"

"We did, but also nothing. They were strange. They zigzagged rather than swirled. Never seen anything like it."

"He can't just appear out of thin air," said Detective Fits. "Check all the birth lists, and immigration lists, and if that's no good, check with the international police."

"Yes, sir," the clerk said, turning to leave. "Oh, and by the way, Alf's parents wondered if we'd drop him off at home. Seems they're having a party and cannot possibly leave."

"Where do they live?"

"Mainsfield."

"Mainsfield! That's six hours drive away!"

"Like I said, sir, they're a little unusual."

"What's their number?" said Detective Sander. "I'll give them unusual."

53 – Parenting Style

Jack and Jill Upton-Hill sat in the police station staring at Alf and Siggy. The boys had spent the night in the jail and hadn't slept well. There were drunks and all sorts in the other cells making noise till early morning. Alf and Siggy had been given a cell by themselves. Now they were sitting in the interrogation room with Detective Sander and Alf's parents.

"I am not leaving without him," said Alf bluntly. "It's Siggy. I always told you he was real, and he is."

"You never said he was a hunchback," said Alf's mum, trying to sound nice.

Siggy gave her a look to kill, but bit his tongue.

"And we can't just take children under our wing willy-nilly," said Alf's dad. "You have to be reasonable."

"He has nowhere to go," pleaded Alf, suddenly feeling how hard it was to be a child on this side. In Instar you were accepted according to your gifts and abilities. Not here. Here you had to have numbers and documents saying who you are and where you were born and who you belong to. If you didn't have those, you were nobody.

"Well, it's fine by me," declared Alf's mum suddenly changing her mind. "If Alf likes him, then we'll take him."

"He looks a little atypical," said Alf's dad. Then he shrugged. "But why not? Yes, let's have him. More the merrier."

Detective Sander sat up, exasperated. "As you stated earlier, Mr Upton-Hill, people can't just take children willy-nilly."

"We changed our mind," said Alf's mum. "I like his hunchback now. It's growing on me." She caught herself, "So to speak, Siggy. No offense."

"You can't have him," said Detective Sander, standing up. "This session is over. Mr and Mrs Upton-Hill, your son is free to leave with you now."

Jack and Jill stood up.

"What about the gold?" asked Jack.

"It'll stay here; it's part of an ongoing investigation."

"And when it's over?" asked Jill.

"The gold cannot be his ... theirs," said Detective Sander.

"And if you cannot prove it?" said Jill.

"Then ... then I'm not sure. We'll let a judge decide."

Jack and Jill signed a few papers and took Alf, kicking and screaming, outside.

"I'm not leaving," he shouted.

"They'll keep him whether you stay here or not," said his dad kindly.

Alf stood on the steps. There were tears in his eyes. He was completely helpless.

* * *

Alf sat on the train and stared out the window. The carriage swayed back and forth and rattled rhythmically. He watched the fields and towns sweep by but didn't pay much attention. His thoughts were on Siggy ... and Mia ... and Cam and Ester and Farlin. They all kept swirling around in his head and he was unconsciously frowning and muttering to himself. A man in a suit sat diagonally across from him in the carriage. He was fiddling with his cell phone but kept glancing at Alf. Alf didn't notice; he'd put his pack on the seat opposite to keep it from being occupied. The train was half empty anyway. He was surprised that his parents hadn't kicked up a fuss. As soon as they got home Alf asked for a few hundred dollars and said he was going back.

"And drop me at the station, too," he demanded.

His mother gave him a look.

"Please," he added, in a pleasant tone.

Alf had been well trained.

They stopped by the supermarket, bought a couple of subs, withdrew money from the bank machine and drove to the station. His father hadn't come.

"See you later, Alf. I have a great idea for a painting," and he rushed upstairs.

Alf's dad wasn't a painter, but Alf had no doubt that he was telling the truth. His parents did what they wanted.

"Bye, Alfred Singworthy Upton-Hill," cooed his mother from the curbside drop-off, oblivious that Alf hated his full name. "Don't forget that school starts on September fifth. That's two days after Labor Day weekend. I'm sure you'll notice how people act differently that weekend. That's when you have to come home. Oh, I forgot," and she rummaged in her handbag. "Here's a cell phone. Take it just in case. I think the battery's dead."

She gave him a slobbery kiss and Alf winced. Love was one thing, but did women have to slobber all over him? He closed the car door and waved and smiled. In his head he was running through the checklist of all the proper things he should be doing. His mom turned and checked for traffic over her left shoulder.

"And thank you," Alf shouted, remembering another item.

She half waved and half turned and frowned at the same time. She didn't like to be distracted while driving, it wasn't her strong suit.

Alf ran through the check list again.

"Love you!" he called out, finally remembering the last item on the list of mother mollification.

The car screeched to a halt. It stuck out into traffic at forty-five degrees and blocked two lanes. Cars were forced to stop. Someone blew their horn. The door flew open and out jumped his mom. Alf's eyes opened in alarm. He thought she'd changed her mind. She ran over.

"Love you too, munchkins," she said, and slobbered on him again.

Then she skipped back to the car and took off with a lurch and a screech. Alf grinned as she vanished into traffic. He checked the cell phone and it was dead. He didn't have a charger either.

The train wound into the hills to Upper Farnon and came to a stop. Alf got out and made his way to the edge of town. He put his thumb out and tried to look harmless. It was the wrong time to be hitchhiking. People were getting out of work and rushing home. Finally, a gruff old codger stopped and let him sit in the back of his pickup along with his pit bull.

"Don't touch him," growled the man.

The dog bared his teeth and growled too. Luckily he was chained.

Alf walked up the rutted path towards the trailer house in the fading light. The lights were out and no cars were around. The only sign of life were the chickens pecking and scratching in the yard. One was sitting on the steering wheel of a junked car. Perhaps Cam's mum had gone shopping. Alf knocked on the door. He didn't expect a reply and didn't get one. He tried the handle. The door was open and he went in. The house was dim and he turned on a light. He checked every room. No one was there. He boiled the last three eggs and ate them with toast. Then he went to bed.

54 – Escape

Cam's mum shook Alf awake the next morning.

"What the hell are you doing here?"

Alf groaned and sat up. "I can't just leave Siggy, or Cam. We're not finished."

"Well, Cam's not shown up and Siggy's flown the coop. So you'd better get up. Breakfast is going to be lousy; someone stole my eggs," and she clouted Alf across the ear, but not too hard.

Alf lay for a moment digesting what she'd said. Somehow it wouldn't register. Then it did. He leaped up and ran to the kitchen.

"What do you mean, 'Siggy's flown the coop'?"

"That's why I came home late last night," said Cam's mum, throwing a stack of cold, greasy, buttered toast onto a plate. "Eat," she said.

Alf sat down. "But ... "

"Eat!"

Alf put a piece of toast in his mouth.

"With jam, you moron," said Cam's mum, shoving an open jam jar with a knife sticking out of it towards him.

Alf dutifully put jam on the toast and took a huge bite.

"Now tell me," he mumbled through his stuffed mouth.

Cam's mum flicked on the electric kettle and sat down. She sighed. She looked tired and grumpy.

"I went to see Siggy a couple of hours after you left. I thought I could do something, or at least speak to him and cheer him up. I went into the police station and asked for him at the desk. The man looked at me. Eyed me like I was a criminal or something. 'Did I do something wrong?' I asked. He turns and goes away. Out comes a smartass detective, Mister Sandypants. Takes me into his office and grills me about Siggy. I told him I thought you two were runaways needing time away from home. What an insulting man. Took my address and said he'd be looking into me and my kind. The skunk."

"But what about Siggy?" said Alf.

"I'm getting to that. Let's have tea."

She heaved herself up and threw a pinch of tea leaves in the pot and poured in hot water. She grabbed two mugs and sat down again.

"Then he said Siggy escaped."

"Escaped!"

Cam's mum nodded. "'How did you lose him?' says I. 'Aren't you the police? Aren't you the ones minded to look after our kids?' Oh, I gave him hell. He was as red in the face as my arse in a sauna."

Alf tried not to think of Cam's mum's derriere in a sauna. "Go on," he said, struggling to swallow his toast.

"Finally he told me what happened, but I had to drag it out of him. Said I'd report him and the whole cop shop to the newspapers and television stations and all his bosses. Anyway, after you'd left, Siggy said he was tired of being inside for so long and could he see the sun and get some fresh air. So they took him to the prison courtyard and he vanished."

"Vanished!" exclaimed Alf.

"That's what I said. Where did he go? Climb the wall? Dig a hole? 'No, no, no,' said the detective, red in the face again. 'Then what then?' asks I. 'He flew over the wall,'" says the detective.

Alf stared at Cam's mum, trying to work it out.

"'Flew over the wall!' says I. 'Are you out of your head and daft?' 'No,' says he, and admits that he was the one who brought Siggy into the courtyard. 'So what happened?' says I. He tells me that he took Siggy out and Siggy says he'd like to jog around. No problem. There's nowhere to go, just a big yard with four walls two stories high and topped with barbwire. So Siggy starts jogging round and round, slowly getting warmed up. Then he whips off his jacket and shirt and instead of a hunchback he has wings and he flies over the wall."

Alf sat with a piece of toast hanging half way to his mouth. He grinned hugely. "That's got to be true," he said. "Only Siggy could do that. I told you he was an elf."

"That's what I thought too," said Cam's mum. "And I'm not too sure about you either," she added, giving Alf a suspicious look. "Anyways, I looked at the detective like *he* was mad, but like I said, I thought it was true. I gave him hell. Said he was crazy and making excuses and had no right to be a policeman and that I'd report him. I said he'd killed Siggy and buried him. I said I'd looked after Siggy like my own son and here he was murdering him and hiding his body. Finally the detective showed me the security video of the courtyard, and there it was. Siggy whips off his shirt, the one I altered for him, and there's no hunchback. There's folded up wings, scrunched up like a newborn butterfly, and they stretch out and he runs and over the wall he goes."

"Yea for Siggy!" shouted Alf leaping up.

"I drove around the town hoping I'd see him or he me. Round and round I went till three in the morning. No sign of him. He'd be a fool to stay in town anyways, with his odd looks and red hair and wings—or a hunchback if he can fold them up again. You'd spot him a mile away."

"So where do you think he went?"

"Looking for you," said Cam's mum. "What else would he do?"

55 – *To and fro*

"Siggy! This is a surprise."

Jack and Jill were weeding their lawn. They'd planted it with dandelions, but grass still managed to find a way in now and then. They'd looked up at the same time to see Siggy standing five feet away. The sight tugged at Jill's heart, with his hunchback and dirty clothes. She immediately wondered if she still had some of Alf's old clothes, but saw that the style wouldn't be right.

"Let's go to the department store," she said.

Siggy looked at her oddly. So did Jack.

"Soda and sandwiches would be better," said Jack. "You two can go shopping later if you like."

"Right, right," said Jill, jumping up. "Just getting ahead of myself."

She stuck out her hand.

"Hello, Siggy. Nice to meet you, again."

Siggy didn't take her hand.

"Where's Alf?" he said.

"Oh, he left," said Jack. "Said he needed to go to Cam's mum's place and try to get you out of jail."

"Drat," said Siggy.

He took Jill's hand and pulled her towards the kitchen.

"I'll take the soda and sandwiches now," he said. "I'm starving. And you're right, I do need a new set of clothes."

"I never said that," said Jill.

"But you thought it. I saw you look at how dirty I was. I'll also need to dye my hair. I thought turquoise would be lovely, wouldn't it? Is your hairdresser any good?"

Alf's dad followed them into the kitchen and made himself and Jill a cup of coffee. They sat at the table, staring at their guest and wondering who he really was.

"So tell us the whole tale," said Jill after she'd made a sandwich.

Siggy gave them a high-speed vignette of all the events since the night they'd brought Alf to the carnival. On the way he left out lots of details.

Jack and Jill hardly believed a word of it, but tried to keep a straight face.

"So how'd you get away from the police?" asked Jack.

"They took me outside and I slipped away when they were off guard," said Siggy. "They don't have a right to keep me anyway. I've don't nothing illegal."

"And how did you get here?" asked Jill.

"I asked a trucker for a lift. Said I was a runaway trying to get home again. He dropped me off about seven miles away and then I fl— ... and then I walked."

"You're welcome to stay as long as you like," said Jack, "but we have to know who you really are. That's only fair."

"I'm Siggy," said Siggy with a sigh.

Alf's mum put her hand on his arm sympathetically.

"Siggy's not real," she said kindly. "I know you're good friends with Alf, and you have this wonderful story, but Alf's got a tremendous imagination and sometimes he lets it run away from him. Tell us who you really are, sweetie."

Siggy gave Jack and Jill an assessing look.

"Fine," he said, "have it your way. What did you see behind Alf's ear when he was born?"

Jill's coffee cup rattled and she sat up. Jack looked at her, his expression changed.

"An elf," said Jack. "I'm sure Alf's mum told him the story."

"Okay," said Siggy. "Who woke you up by pulling the covers off your bed and shouting that Alf was suffocating?"

Jack and Jill were quiet. They were remembering how Alf's head had gotten tangled in his bed cover in his crib.

"And who led Jack to him when Alf was lost on that picnic. Who kept saying, 'This way. This way'? And who made his tire swing go round faster and faster when it should have gone slower and slower? And which part of the garden did you two secretly—"

"I think I believe you," said Jill quickly. She stared at Siggy in wonder.

"Well, I'll be darned," said Jack. "I'll be darned."

"So now you have a 'real' body, but have lost your magic," said Jill.

"Yes," said Siggy, "though I do have one last thing."

"Which is?"

Siggy stood up and took off his jacket and shirt. Then he turned and opened his wings.

* * *

The phone rang. And rang. Then rang some more. No one answered because Siggy and Alf's parents were on the freeway to Upper Farnon.

"No one's in," said Alf. "I've tried ten times now. It's been hours. They must have gone away."

"Keep trying," said Cam's mum. "Maybe they went shopping."

The Darkling Beasts

"Never for that long."

"Maybe they went shopping and then for a walk and then were in the garden and then out to a restaurant."

"That's pushing it," said Alf.

"Keep trying anyway."

Alf sighed. Cam's mum was a killer to argue with.

"So how are we going to get the Hall of Mirrors back?" he asked, changing the subject.

"I'm thinking," said Cam's mum.

"You're watching TV."

"That's how I think. It's intellectually engaging."

Alf propped his head in his hands. It was no use. He grabbed his cap, went outside, and slammed the door. It was drizzling and cool. The weather in Upper Farnon was changeable. One minute this, one minute that. He walked along the driveway towards the road. The driveway sloped gently and maple trees lined the north side. Half rotten split rail fences ran along both sides. Beyond, meadows curved away to woodland.

Alf wanted to get the Hall of Mirrors back, but Cam's mum insisted it was Cam's business. Nevertheless, she was pondering something, that was for sure. She hadn't said much and wore a frown. That had to mean something.

The road came in sight through the maple trees. The part he saw curved away down the hill. A car was pulled in on the verge. One man sat inside, another stood by the opened door and scanned Cam's mum's place with binoculars. They'd see most of it from where they were. Just part of the trailer home and some of the driveway would be concealed. That's why they hadn't seen him yet.

Alf stopped and watched. He didn't think much of it at first but the man in the car spoke to the man outside. He immediately turned the binoculars towards Alf.

"That's odd," thought Alf.

He casually continued his walk down the driveway, but scanned the area without being obvious about it. Then he spotted him. There, on the far edge of the meadow to the left, partly hidden by the split rail fence, was another man also watching him. He had binoculars, plus a cell phone to his ear. Alf must have looked too intently; when he looked back the man was gone and the car was pulling away. Alf bent low and ran towards the road. He heard the car pass the junction, stop and quickly go on. By the time he got to the junction the road was clear. He returned to the house, looking back every now and then.

"I saw three men looking at your place," he said when he got into the house. "They acted suspiciously. Two had binoculars. They left once they knew I'd seen them."

Cam's mum looked up. She stared blankly at him for a moment.

"What?" she said, her eyes glazed over. She'd been watching TV for hours.

"Men. I said men were watching the place."

"Oh, those guys. I think they want to date me."

"They were acting suspiciously," said Alf.

"All men act suspiciously around single women," said Cam's mum. "Just you wait till you grow up, you'll see."

They heard a car coming up the driveway. For a huge woman, Cam's mum moved with incredible speed. A moment later she appeared from her bedroom with a shotgun in her hand. She pumped it and flicked off the safety.

"Get under my bed," she ordered. "And don't come out until I tell you to."

Her tone left no room for argument. Alf ran to her room and dived under the bed. It was dirty in the extreme and huge dust balls rolled around. A massive pair of knickers, left there decades ago by the look of it, kept him company. He tried not to see them.

The car stopped. Doors opened and closed.

"Now that's a fine head of hair if ever I saw one," boomed Cam's mum. "I think I'll try one myself, if you won't get jealous."

Alf relaxed. Must be friends. Then he heard him.

"Where's Alf?" said Siggy.

Alf was out like a shot, racing through the house and out the door. There stood his parents with Cam's mum, shotgun casually resting on her shoulder, and Siggy, with new clothes and bright turquoise hair, was running towards him with his arms open.

56 – Burning

"That's quite a gun you have," said Jack. "Do you always greet visitors with it?"

They were all in the kitchen waiting for the kettle to boil.

"Only if they're men who want to bother me," said Cam's mum, giving him a look. "I don't like to be bothered."

Jack opened his mouth to say something, but changed his mind.

"Those are lovely curtains you have," said Jill, trying to make small talk.

"Those? Trash if there ever was. Thrift stores are going to hell."

Alf and Siggy grinned, then burst out in laughter.

"And what's so funny about that?" said Cam's mum. "Get out of my house this minute and let us adults have a real conversation. Out!"

She took a step towards them as Alf and Siggy, still laughing helplessly, bolted for the door. Siggy almost made it out unscathed but was hit in the back of the head with the wet dish sponge. He tripped and fell on the deck with a thud. Jill jumped up, but Cam's mum slammed the door and slipped the lock.

"Brats," she said. "Who the hell brought them up?"

That was the last Alf and Siggy heard. They were laughing too hard to hear any more.

"I'd love to have seen your mum's face," said Siggy, holding his sides and bending over.

They settled down and wandered up towards the barn and chicken coop. It was dusk and the chickens had gone inside. Alf peeked into the coop. Except for a couple of broody hens sitting on their nests, the chickens were lined up on the roosts. Some already had their heads under their wings. He locked the door and they went to the pole barn and sat on an old hay rig.

"We're being watched," said Alf, and he told Siggy what he had seen.

"Could be us they're interested in, but unlikely," said Siggy. "Why would they be? We're kids. You left the police station with your parents and I escaped in a way I doubt they'll advertise. They're probably looking for Cam. It could be detectives."

"Could," said Alf. "Except they acted like they didn't want to be seen."

"We'll just have to be careful," said Siggy. "Got any ideas about getting the Hall back?"

"No," said Alf. "Cam's the one that needs to renew the license plates and pay a fine. If he shows up at the pound they'll arrest him."

"Won't he get a surprise if he walks through the Hall and see's he's at the pound," said Siggy. "Well, it's not the end of the world."

"That's easy for you to say," snorted Alf. "He might have to go to court and spend time in jail. And they'll never believe him if he tells the truth about where he got the gold."

A car climbed the hill and slowed down. It turned into the driveway. It was a police car, it's headlights probing the drizzle in the half-light. Alf and Siggy dropped off the hay rig and darted behind an old tractor. The car stopped and Cam's mum came out of the house. They said something to her and she started berating them. The policemen didn't react much. They just shrugged their shoulders and went back to the car. One of them opened the boot, took out a cardboard box, and handed it to Cam's mum. They tipped their hats, got in and drove off.

Alf and Siggy raced down the hill and into the house. Cam's mum stood in the kitchen looking pale. The box sat on the table, and Jack and Jill were standing to one side looking uncertain.

"What's wrong?" asked Alf.

"It's the Hall," she said. "It burnt. Completely. They don't know how. They think it was arson."

She sat down on a chair.

"Oh, yes," she added, pushing the box towards them. "The man in the car pound found Kitty-o. Heard her mewing inside and let her out. The Hall went up in flames an hour later. Lucky her, she might have fried."

57 - *Lawyer*

Alf and his parents picked up the gold at the police station, or at least Alf's part. They'd found a lawyer in town and he'd applied to the court for the immediate return of personal belongings impounded by the police without cause. The judge said that barring any charges of theft or reasonable suspicion thereof all personal property belonged to Alf; rags or riches made no difference. Detective Sander handed over the bullion personally with a sour, puzzled, perplexed and petulant look on his face. Siggy had been wisely left at Cam's mum's place.

"Where's that redheaded kid?" he'd asked.

Everyone shrugged. "We don't know where that redheaded kid is," they replied truthfully, the image of Siggy's bright turquoise hair flashing through their minds.

Once Alf's gold was safely collected they'd gone back to the lawyer. Siggy's gold, it seemed, was a different matter. Because Siggy had no records—no birth certificate, no school attendance, no passport, no nothing—he didn't exist, at least not legally. And if you don't exist legally, then you can't claim something belongs to you when you can't prove that you are who you say you are. If Siggy really wanted the gold he'd have to get his parents to register him, but they'd get hell for not doing so in the first place. Or, if he didn't have parents and he was an orphan, he'd be farmed out to foster parents if he tried to register. And no, it would not be easy for Jack and Jill to acquire Siggy as their foster son.

So that took care of that.

On the other hand, said the lawyer, if he waits until he's eighteen he can state he was abandoned as a child, get his papers and claim the gold. The state will, of course, do everything in its power to track down his wayward parents. His advice for Siggy (if Jack and Jill knew his whereabouts) was to write a notarized claim on the gold and have the notary deliver the claim by hand to the police station and receive a signature of receipt. He was to state that the gold was his, to include the time and date and circumstances of the gold being taken from him by the police, and then state he'd come to collect it when he was eighteen. That way the gold would have to be held and not, ahem, 'lost' in the system, if you know what I mean. By the time Jack and Jill left his office the lawyer was giving them doubtful looks, but kept his mouth shut because they paid him in cash, no receipt needed.

"So where do you sell gold?" asked Alf when they got back to Cam's mum's place.

"A gold dealer," said Siggy. "Duh!"

He was grumpy because he didn't get his gold back. Not that he cared; it was the principle of the thing.

"Well, there's not one here in Upper Farnon, that's for sure," said Cam's mum. "Not that I've ever tried to sell gold. Ain't got none except my wedding band, and it's silver. New York would be my guess. There's so many people in that town that one or two of them must be gold dealers."

"That's an idea," said Jill. "We have to go there next week anyway."

"But what about Cam?" asked Alf. "He's stuck in Instar."

"He's a grown man," said Cam's mum. "Let him live there. Less work for me. Lazy sod, I'm fed up with him being under foot. Where's the remote?" and she turned on the TV and raised the volume to full blast.

"Looks like it's time to go," said Jill, taking the hint.

"Where's Kitty-o?" said Siggy, and he and Alf ran off to find her.

Ten minutes later they came back with her slung over Alf's shoulder. She was half the size of him when stretched out. He put her in the back seat of the car.

"We'd better say goodbye," said Alf, and he stuck his head in the kitchen door. "We're leaving," he shouted.

The TV turned off and Cam's mum lumbered outside.

"Good riddance," she said.

Jack and Jill looked shocked, but Alf and Siggy threw their arms around her.

"Bye," they said. "See you later."

"My arse," said Cam's mum, wiping away a tear. "Bloody fly got in my eye."

She turned and went back into the house and the TV blared back on.

58 – A new Nest

"Show us your wings," said Alf. "Why didn't you tell me you had them? Here I was, thinking you were a hunchback and I couldn't work out why."

Siggy looked shy.

"You're not shy, are you?" said Alf. "Not Siggy—no way! Look, we're here in my bedroom and my parents have gone out. What's to hide?"

Siggy blushed.

"You are shy," said Alf gently.

"A bit," said Siggy.

"But why? I think wings would be wonderful. I'd love a pair myself, and you showed them to my parents."

"I had to," said Siggy. "They were not believing who I was."

Siggy stood still for a moment. "It's just that they're not like my real wings," he said, "the ones I have when I'm a real elf are so different. So much, much better."

"I've seen those," said Alf, "and they are beautiful, or at least when you're in a good mood."

Siggy thought for a moment. "There's no harm, I suppose," he said at last. He took off his shirt and turned. There on his upper back, where the shoulder blades are, were Siggy's wings. They looked like soft, crumpled fabric. Then they opened. They unfurled as if inflated from within. It happened quickly and Alf gasped. They shifted from flesh color to pale blue with a delicate, iridescent sheen. Then they changed to yellow, and again to blue. Siggy turned and fluttered them. The room became a whirlwind and shook the posters on the walls and sent papers flying. A moment later they were folded up and Siggy put his shirt back on.

Alf was stunned.

"I wish Mia was here to see this," was all he could say.

* * *

Jack and Jill went up the hill to fetch the boys and scold them. They were running around the well at the top and screaming their heads off. They were letting off steam. They were only kids, after all—or at least Alf was. Siggy's age didn't compute somehow. One minute he acted like a real kid, the next he was discussing the latest in computer technology with Jack. Jack had fancied himself a bit of an expert on the subject until he had a conversation with Siggy. Now he listened and asked questions.

"Alf! Siggy! Stop it! Come here! It says don't walk on the grass!"

The boys ran over. They were out of breath and panting. They'd gone into Mainsfield to do business and dropped the boys at the park.

"Let's go to the bank," said Jack, heading down the hill to the car. "Then we'll have lunch."

They drove into the town center and parked near their bank. They'd decided to put some of the gold into a safe deposit box. The rest would be sold to a gold dealer in New York.

"We'd like to rent a safe deposit box," said Jill to the teller, and they were led to a separate cubby. A young banker's assistant came over and helped them fill out the forms.

"What size will you want?" asked the assistant, showing them a chart with all the options.

"Not too big," said Jack, taking out one of the gold slugs from his briefcase. "We're going to put in ten of these."

The assistant's eyes opened in surprise, but said nothing. He measured the slug and pointed to a box size that would hold them.

"We'll take that one, then," said Jack.

"Whose name will it be in?" asked the assistant.

"All four of us," said Jill.

The assistant eyed Alf and Siggy.

"If the kids are under eighteen they can only access it with you present," he said. "Sorry, it's the law."

Jack and Jill looked at the boys. They shrugged. What was there to do?

"That's fine," said Jack. "Just make sure their names are on the form."

When they'd finished the assistant led them into the vault and gave them the key. The vault door was huge. It was two feet thick with layer upon layer of polished steel and locking mechanisms. Inside was a narrow passage lined with dozens of numbered metal doors of all sizes. The assistant showed them their box and said he'd step out for a minute. They were loading the slugs when another man came in. Siggy hissed quietly and stepped behind Alf's parents.

"Ah, Mr and Mrs Upton-Hill, a pleasure to see you," the man beamed, and shook hands with them. "And are these your children? Delightful! I'm Mr Gard, the bank manager," he said to Alf.

Alf took his proffered hand and smiled politely.

"I'm Alf," he said. He felt uneasy. He had no idea why Siggy had reacted so vehemently.

"And who is this other young chap?" the manager asked. "Must be shy if he's hiding."

The Darkling Beasts

"This is Alf's friend, Siggy," said Jill, stepping out of the way. "He's staying with us at the moment."

Siggy stared warily and didn't take the banker's hand.

"He is a little shy," said Jill, making an excuse.

The banker didn't smile. He glanced at Siggy's bare feet, then turned and eyed the gold.

"That's quite a haul you have, Mr and Mrs Upton-Hill," he said, "quite a haul," and he reached into the box and took a slug out. "My gosh, wherever did you get these?"

He quickly raised his hand.

"I'm so sorry. A bank is never to ask questions. My apologies. I just happened to come by and saw you."

He raised the slug to his nose and sniffed it.

"Well, must rush," he said suddenly. "Pleasure to meet you all," and he left the vault.

"Siggy!" chided Jill. "There's no need to be rude. He's a very nice man."

Siggy said nothing.

They finished filling the box and left the bank. Siggy was quiet the whole way home. Alf was still uneasy, though he couldn't put his finger on why he felt that way. It was as if a shadow had insinuated itself between the earth and the sun.

"What was that about?" said Alf as soon as they were alone.

"Didn't you see?" said Siggy. "That was one of them."

* * *

New York hustled and bustled. The buildings crowded in and soared. To Alf they looked like giant crystals.

"See—they're moving," said Siggy, pointing upwards.

Alf looked up. Clouds were scudding across the sky and the buildings seemed to move too. For a moment he became giddy.

They were staying in a hotel in Chinatown. Alf's parents had gone to a gold dealer and the boys decided to wander about. They caught the subway to Bowling Green and walked in Battery Park. They gazed across at the Statue of Liberty. They were going there in the afternoon with Alf's parents. After a while Siggy wanted to see more of the city.

They walked up Broadway, trying to imagine how it must have looked as an Indian trail hundreds of years ago. Soon, men in perfectly cut business suits and expensive sunglasses were everywhere. Siggy fell silent. They turned onto Wall Street. Alf didn't need to ask Siggy what he was seeing. He knew too, and the hair on the back of his neck was rising. The cockroaches were everywhere.

Rate it: if you enjoyed this tale,
please, next time you're on Amazon,
give it a couple of words + as many stars as
your enjoyment.
The biggest challenge to an author
is promotion, and what people see on the big river
definitely makes a difference.
Thank you ~ Reg Down

~ Children's Books by Reg Down ~

Please visit *www.tiptoes-lightly.net* for updates, sample stories from the books and many free tales for parents and teachers

The Tales of Tiptoes Lightly

The Festival of Stones
Autumn and Winter Tales of Tiptoes Lightly

Big-Stamp Two-Toes the Barefoot Giant
Spring Tales of Tiptoes Lightly

The Magic Knot ~ and other tangles!
A comedy starring Pine Cone and Pepper Pot and the lovely Tiptoes Lightly

The Lost Lagoon
Adventures of Greenleaf the Sailor and Tiptoes Lightly

The Bee who Lost his Buzz
(The illustrated color book of the first part of The Tales of Tiptoes Lightly — especially suitable for younger children)

The Cricket and the Shepherd Boy
A Christmas Tale

The Starry Bird
An Easter Tale

Sir Gillygad and the Gruesome Egg
A Tale for Nines to Twelves (or so)

Eggs for the Hunting
An Easter tale starring Pine Cone and Pepper Pot and the illimitable Tiptoes Lightly

The Midsummer Mouse
Midsummer Tales of Tiptoes Lightly and the Summer Queen

The Treasure Cave
Sea Tales of Tiptoes Lightly

Adam's Alphahet
(A unique alphabet tale)

The Adventures of Jayne
~ the cat who was a dog

The Nine Lives of Pinrut the Turnip Boy
(A tale for eights to twelves)

The Darkling Beasts
(For grade 5 to high school)

King Red and the white Snow
A picture book of color tales

A Tangle of Tales
Stories for Children

The Alphabet
How Pine Cone and Pepper Pot (with the help of Tiptoes Lightly and Farmer John) learned Tom Nutcracker and June Berry their alphabet.

The Seven Saws of Speedy Weedy and Mosey Dawdle
and other tales of wisdom and nonsense

Translations

Los Cuentos de Puntitas de Pies
(Spanish translation of The Tales of Tiptoes Lightly)

La Abeja que Peridó su Zumbido
(Spanish translation of The Bee who lost his Buzz)

El Grillo y el Joven Pastor: Cuento de Navidad
(Spanish translation of The Cricket and the Shepherd Boy)

Die Geschichten der Elfe Leichtfuß
(German translation of The Tales of Tiptoes Lightly)

Das Bienchen das sein Summ' verlor
(German translation of The Bee who lost his Buzz)

~ Books for Grown-Ups ~

The Fetching of Spring
A novel
"... an excellent pick ..." **Midwest Book Review**

"... wonderful reading of the very best sort: a story true and strong, told with joy and wonder, clarity and hope. This one is not to be missed."
Nancy Parsons, Waldorf Books

Leaving Room for the Angels
Eurythmy and the Art of Teaching
AWSNA Publishing

"This is a remarkable book! The first section should be read by all Waldorf teachers. It contains wisdom and practical advice that will benefit every teacher."
David Mitchell,
Editor in Chief, AWSNA Publications

Color and Gesture
The Inner Life of Color

"My highest praise and appreciation go to Reg Down for these quiet, sensitive, lucid and lyrical pages. ... It is my hope that representatives from many of the arts and humanities will seek out and learn something profound from Mr. Down's imaginative work. Reg Down is a master of witnessing."
Therese Schroeder-Sheker,
academic dean, School of Music-Thanatology
Chalice of Repose Project

~ Selected Reviews of the Children's Books ~

The Tales of Tiptoes Lightly: "I wish there was something like this when my two children were growing up. It's a wonderful book." **Book Review Cafe**

The Tales of Tiptoes Lightly: "Our preschooler hasn't been a big chapter-book fan, but she routinely asked for another Tiptoes Story. Borrow or buy? Buy! It's a great way to introduce the chapter book concept to young readers and will be a book that middle-readers will enjoy a second (or third) time around." **The Reading Tub Review**

The Tales of Tiptoes Lightly: "Fabulous book! This is an amazing, wonderful, peaceful book! It's just so simple and lovely. My daughter's had these books since she was 3; she's now 7 and still loves them. I will save them for my grandchildren!" **Amazon Review**

The Festival of Stones: "This is a fascinating book by an extraordinarily imaginative writer." **The Reading Tub Review**

The Festival of Stones: "Another good one! We love Tiptoes and her friends! Great book! I would recommend this for 6-9 year olds." **Amazon Review**

Big-Stamp Two-Toes the Barefoot Giant: "The adventures of Tiptoes and her friends are a constant request from my three-year-old son and seven-year-old daughter at storytime. They are timeless and are due to be classic children's stories." **Amazon Review**

Big-Stamp Two-Toes the Barefoot Giant: "Love it! We have read all of the Tiptoes series and would HIGHLY recommend them to any child. Reg Down has done a fantastic job and my favorite part is they are so original. I feel like these stories are classics that I will keep for my grandchildren." **Amazon review**

The Magic Knot: "This book is a must-have for any child, right along with all of Reg Down's books. We have read this book many times and you will not be disappointed." **Amazon Review**

The Magic Knot: "Wonderful! Great book! My girls ages 7 & 10 both loved it.." *Amazon Review*

"The Lost Lagoon is a fun and recommended pick for younger readers." **Midwest Book Review**

The Lost Lagoon: "These stories are fun and I love how they work along with the seasons and nature around us." **Amazon Review**

The Cricket and the Shepherd Boy: "Who but Reg Down could bring us a new Christmas story that glows with such warmth and beauty? *The Cricket and the Shepherd Boy* is a gift for the Season of Love ... it will live on in the hearts of the children and adults who hear it. *The Cricket and the Shepherd Boy* is a treasure." **Nancy Parsons, Waldorf Books**

"Also highly recommended is Reg Down's *The Cricket and The Shepherd Boy*, a touching holiday story that brings the generous and reverent spirit of Christmas to life year-round." **Midwest Book Review**

The Bee who Lost his Buzz: "Each warmhearted mini-tale blends into the next, making *The Bee Who Lost His Buzz* flow into a captivating whole. *The Bee Who Lost His Buzz* is ideal for teaching children how much fun reading can be." **Midwest Book Review**

The Starry Bird: "... the perfect book to send along with a favorite young person on their spring vacation or in their Easter basket." **Midwest Book Review**

The Starry Bird: "Best Easter Gift! The Easter Bunny left this book in the girl's Easter Basket last year and it was by far the most treasured gift ... even above the chocolate bunny!" **Amazon Review**

Eggs for the Hunting: "If you aren't a Tiptoes fan yet, *Eggs for the Hunting*, the seventh book in the Tiptoes Tales, is a great place to start. It's a wonderful book for young children, highly imaginative and utterly entertaining." **Waldorf Today**

The Treasure Cave: ""Reg Down has done it again in his unique style—magnificently imaginative and utterly entertaining. A heart-warming gift to families to help find a new meaning in Thanksgiving through the wonder of Tiptoes Lightly. Five Stars!" **Waldorf Today**

The Treasure Cave: ""A deftly crafted novel by an experienced and talented author and illustrator of books for children ... superbly drawn characters and thoroughly engaging storyline. Wonderfully entertaining" **Midwest Book Review**

"A Tangle of Tales is a great "read-aloud" repository for homeroom, storytime, bedtime, or the simple joy of parent-child reading time - highly recommended." *Midwest Book Review*

A Tangle of Tales: "Always wonderful stories: My children love Reg's books and this is no exception! If you want lovely child friendly stories, then look no further." *Amazon review*

The Midsummer Mouse: "A modern fairytale certain to delight young readers (and their parents!) ... an engaging world of fantasy and enchantment, gladness and jollity, mystery and misadventure, and great fun from beginning to end ... enthusiastically recommended for children ages 5 through 10." *Midwest Book Review*

The Midsummer Mouse: "Reg Down is a masterful storyteller! An unbroken stream of unbridled imagination - just what children (and their parents) need now. If you're not a Tiptoes fan, this is your chance to get on board." *David Kennedy, Waldorf Today*

The Midsummer Mouse: "A classic children's tale in the making! My family and I really enjoy the Tiptoes Lightly books and this one did not disappoint. In fact, I think it may be the best of the series, if not one of the best children's books ever written. I was full of wonder and laughing just as much as my children. After we finished, my son wanted it read to him again and I was more than happy to oblige." *Amazon Review*

Adam's Alphabet: " ... continues to document (Reg Down's) impressive storytelling talents. Exceptionally entertaining and original ..." *Midwest Book Review*

Adam's Alphabet: "My children and I really enjoyed this story ... not so much a beginner's intro to the letters, as a deepening of the experience of the letters, more for the over-7 child. Reg Down has such a gift for stories that seem simple on the surface, yet have layers of meaning waiting to be discovered." *Amazon Review*

The Nine Lives of Pinrut the Turnip Boy: " ... Reg Down again demonstrates a lively imagination combined with superbly crafted storytelling skills that will engage and entertain young readers ranging from grade 3 to grade 6. Very highly recommended ..." *Midwest Book Review*

The Nine Lives of Pinrut the Turnip Boy: "Lovely book! My 6 yr old loves this book and hasn't put it down since she received it as a gift! She is an advanced reader (1st grader reading at a 3rd grade level) and it can be hard to find books that are age appropriate but advanced enough to challenge her and keep her interested in reading. She loves all of Reg Down's books and this is no exception. Great story that is entertaining to children and adults!" *Amazon Review*

The Adventures of Jayne: the cat who was a dog: "Jayne is strong and flawed and funny and ridiculous. My 10 year old and 6 year old children love the book as does their 63 year old grandmother. Charming, charming tales." *Amazon Review*

The Adventures of Jayne: the cat who was a dog: "An entertaining read! I bought this book to read to my five year old daughter and we both loved it. I frequently travel for work, and call or Skype to her to read something at bedtime. I go through a lot of books this way and am always on the lookout for good new books. This one was a pleasure. Fun, silly, and inventive." *Amazon Review*

The Adventures of Jayne: the cat who was a dog: "Hilarious reading! My children loved having this book read to me. It started out as a book for my 6 year old, but my 8 year old could not resist coming and sitting in my lap as well. The book is really funny, with the kids both laughing frequently. The book is also extremely well written. The vocabulary in the book is fantastic and the story flows beautifully." *Amazon Review*

Sir Gillygad and the Gruesome Egg: "What a fabulous story. I read it aloud to our almost 9 year old, and he loved it, and I thoroughly enjoyed reading it too ... the characters are engaging, quirky, whimsical, and a few times amusingly baffling. Highly recommended." *Amazon Review*

Sir Gillygad and the Gruesome Egg: "These stories really are well-written. They cause the reader to use their imagination and to really think; not just read pointless words. Great for bedtime to create a relaxing atmosphere, but not boring!" *Amazon Review*

The Seven Saws of Speedy Weedy and Mosey Dawdle: " ... an impressive and unfailingly entertaining collection of 26 stories specifically written for children from kindergarten through the fourth grade. Perfect for family bedtime story hours or rainy day family entertainment ... very highly recommended for family, school, and community library collections." *Midwest Book Review*

The Alphabet:
how Pine Cone and Pepper Pot
(with the help of Tiptoes Lightly and Farmer John)
learned
Tom Nutcracker and June Berry their letters

"*The Alphabet* is very highly recommended and is as subtly educational as it is sheer fun!" *Midwest Book Review*

The Alphabet: "If **Waldorf Today** awarded a Children's Book of the Year, *The Alphabet* would be the hands-down choice for 2015! Reg Down is the author of the highly successful Tiptoes Lightly series (and) this treasure may be his finest to date. Every page has been colorfully illustrated and will delight his readers. *The Alphabet* lends itself to reading night after night (or lesson after lesson) and is as much at home in a classroom as in a child's library." **Waldorf Today**

The Alphabet: "This book is delightful! We have a couple other Reg Down books, and this is a great addition to our collection. I have 3 boys (8, 5, 2) and they have enjoyed this book a lot!! Lots of laughter and smiles!" **Amazon Review**

The Alphabet: "As huge fans this book does not disappoint. Great story with beautiful illustrations. A much-have for your personal library." **Amazon Review**

The Alphabet: "Captivating story. One of my favorite Waldorf homeschool tools to date." **Amazon Review**

Made in United States
Troutdale, OR
12/06/2023